CONTENTS

PREFACE

Dedicated to my grandchildren - Ruby and Sonny - for their support whilst writing this book.

All illustrations designed and created by the author.

CHAPTER 1: FAIRWAY FARM

The heavens opened and the rains came down with a vengeance. For five days and nights it continually pounded the earth of the Somerset Levels. The rivers that gently meandered through the meadows in the summer were transformed into raging torrents, as the tremendous surge of water powering its way down the surrounding hills filled them along with the dykes. Unable to contain the force of the water, the riverbanks collapsed, submerging the crops growing in the meadows under a lake of thick, brown, muddy water.

Macky had perched himself on the edge of a bale of hay, carefully positioned at the entrance to the old barn. Lifting his head up, he gazed at the grey leaden skies from below the rim of his peaked cap. "When is this damn rain going to stop?" he asked himself.

Looking back across the farmyard he was surprised to see Farmer Brown approaching him, splashing his way through the numerous puddles. The old farmer was dressed for the weather in his bright yellow Macintosh with a Sou'wester clamped to his head and wearing his best green wellington boots.

"Terrible weather Macky," he shouted, over the noise of the beating raindrops. "Yes sir. I've never known it rain for so long," Macky replied. Farmer Brown nodded, and droplets of rainwater fell from his Sou'wester onto his nose. "I'm sorry Macky," he said with a heavy heart, "but I'm afraid that I'll have to let you go."

Macky stared at the farmer with a quizzical look on his face.

Farmer Brown continued, "all my crops are rotting in the fields under a lake of muddy water. I can't save them now and it'll be impossible to bring in the harvest." Macky was stunned. No words of comfort could help the farmer. He just looked at him with pity in his eyes.

"You can stay tonight Macky, but you'll have to go in the morning." As he spoke, he pressed a roll of damp pound notes into Macky's open hand. Macky nodded with gratitude. Farmer Brown was a broken man as he waded back across the farmyard to his house. There would be no money coming in this season and now he was facing ruin.

Young Tom had witnessed the whole scene from his bedroom window. Sitting on his rickety old wooden stool with elbows firmly planted on his bedroom window ledge, head cupped in his hands and nose pressed against the glass, he had a good view of the farmyard. With his index finger he had casually drawn a matchstick figure on the mist forming on the windowpane from his warm breath. To get a better view he had quickly wiped the windowpane with the sleeve of his bright blue cardigan, kindly knitted for him by Aunty Nellie, obliterating the small stickman.

Tom had seen the tramp move the bale of dry hay from within the barn and carefully place it at the entrance. He was wearing a long, dark green trench coat with brass buttons running down its front. A bright red scarf hung from his neck covering part of a long black beard. A dark brown woolly peaked cap adorned his head.

Seated on the bale with his legs dangling down the side, he had carefully removed his sunglasses, glanced up at Tom's bedroom window in the farmhouse and had given him a salute with his right hand. Tom had saluted back. It was then that he had noticed his uncle, Farmer Brown, splashing his way across the farmyard towards the tramp. The farmer had reached the tramp and waved his arms in the air, pointing his hand up to the sky. After a short discussion with the tramp, Tom had noticed him press something into the tramp's hand and then turn to wander wearily back to the farmhouse.

Tom heard the farmhouse door slam closed. He shot out of his bedroom and slid down the banister rail, completely misjudging his landing and ended bottom down on the flagged kitchen floor. "Ouch," he shouted as the pain shot through his body.

"Glad you found the time to honour us with your presence, Tom," muttered his mother, as she stood at the large kitchen table, working a lump of dough into a perfect ball with her long slender fingers.

"Leave him alone Mary. You know what young boys are like," remarked Auntie Nellie, sitting within inches of a roaring fire, rocking slowly in a tired old armchair, whilst her knitting needles clicked out a slow metallic rhythm.

Tom slowly lifted himself up from the stone floor, frantically rubbing his behind. He limped over to the kitchen table and picked up the empty mixing bowl, sliding his finger into the remains of the dough lying in the bottom of the bowl. "What are you baking mum?" he asked, sticking his finger into his mouth, and licking the sweet, doughy paste off it. "Now stop doing that Tom. You know that's a dirty habit," she scolded. "For your information we're having scones for dessert tonight. That's if you let me get on with it!" she exclaimed.

Tom turned to see Farmer Brown shuffle into the kitchen from the hall. He paused at the door and shook himself vigorously, like a shaggy dog that had just swum across a river. Raindrops sprayed across the kitchen floor from his wet Macintosh. His usual smiley face was now no more as he reflected on his talk with Macky.

His pale blue, watery eyes looked sad and his small, white moustache, tucked below a red bulbous nose covered with purple veins, twitched as he felt the warm heat from the kitchen fire. His face bore the tell-tale features of a heavy drinker. He told friends who asked of his health that he only took a small tumbler of brandy every evening for medicinal purposes. He omitted to mention the bottles of brandy tucked away behind the bales of hay in the old barn which kept him going during a heavy day working. He threw off his wellington boots and casually removed his Macintosh. Then he lifted the sou'wester from his head revealing a tatty old flat cap.

Tom glanced at the flat cap. In his opinion the cap was welded to his Uncle Billy's head, for he had never ever seen him without it on. He giggled to himself as he imagined his uncle lying in his bed with the flat cap perched on his head.

"You look glum Billy. That's not like you. Now whatever is the problem lad?" asked Auntie Nellie, with concern in her voice.

Uncle Billy stood motionless as he looked at the scene unfolding before him in the kitchen. His younger sister Mary opened the oven door in the old black leaded cooking range and slid in the scones on a metal tray. The single naked light bulb hanging over the kitchen table cast long shadows into every corner. Her dark brown hair pulled tightly into plaits and the long blue apron gave her an air of professionalism. A silver chain around her neck bore a small Saint Christopher medallion, which swung casually as she went about her work.

Sitting close to the roaring fire, his wife Nellie was busily knitting a long red and white striped scarf for Tom. Her grey hair was tied up in a bun under a black hair net, her ankle length black skirt smouldering at the hem from the fire's intense heat as she hummed a little tune to herself.

Tom unsuccessfully tried to brush the remains of the flour from the kitchen table into a waste bin, spilling most of it onto the floor.

Uncle Billy gave a loud cough to draw their attention. They slowly turned to him with anxious looks on their faces.

"I feel terrible," he stammered into the silence. He paused while he removed his flat cap and carefully folded it in his hand.

Mary and Nellie looked dismayed, for they realised in that

instance he was the bearer of bad news.

The last time he removed his flat cap he had to tell his sister Mary that her husband John had been reported missing, presumed dead while fighting in the war. With a shaking hand he had held the fateful telegram which had been sent from the War Office. He continued. "I've had to tell the tramp that we no longer require his help, because the rain has ruined all the crops. He's been the best worker I've ever employed on the farm, and I'll be really sorry to see him go."

Recovering quickly, Nellie spoke softly to Billy. "It's not your fault Billy. You can't control the weather dear; these things happen, we have just got to get on with life."

"But that's the problem Nellie," Billy replied, his voice rising to a crescendo, "you don't understand. We're ruined," he shouted, whereupon he fell to his knees, hands together in prayer. "Oh, my Lord, please help us. Without the crops we won't have anything to harvest and no money to see us through the winter."

"The Lord's not going to help you now Billy Brown," scolded Auntie Nellie. "You need to be praying that the bank manager will give you a loan. Get up now, you are a silly old sausage."

Mary stood beside Tom, gripping his hand so tightly that he let out a tiny squeal. "Don't worry Billy," she said. "I'll go back to work at the village grocer's shop. I'm sure they will have me back now that the war is over, and things are getting back to normal."

"No, No, I can't have you doing that Sis, you need to be home with Tom now that he hasn't got a father," Billy replied.

"Yes, I understand that, but this is an emergency. After all, Tom was only a baby when we lost his father. We've been living with you and Nellie since we had that terrible news. You are both his family now. He's never known his father."

"Ok then," replied Billy, reluctantly holding up his arms, "I give up. But first thing tomorrow I'll go to see my bank manager and ask him for a loan. It'll be just until we can get on our feet again. If he says yes, then you stay at home with Tom. Do you agree?" Mary nodded reluctantly.

CHAPTER 2: NETHER POPPIT JUNIOR SCHOOL

"I'm worried, in fact, I'm really, really, worried," muttered Tom, as he lay on his bed staring at the ceiling. He hadn't been able to sleep, tossing and turning on the bed, unable to stop the thoughts racing around his brain. The conversation in the kitchen that evening between his mum and Uncle Billy had really upset him.

Aunty Nellie told him that if he could not get to sleep, then he should close his eyes and imagine sheep jumping over a fence, counting each one in turn. He had tried this, but to no avail, so now he started to count the small yellow flowers printed on the wallpaper of his bedroom ceiling.

He had just reached up to number 46 when he heard a gentle tap on his bedroom door. Mary slowly pushed the door open and peered into the room. "For heaven's sake Tom, are you not asleep yet? It's school tomorrow and you need a good night's sleep." "I'm really worried mum. Will we have to leave the farmhouse? I love living with Uncle Billy and Aunty Nellie."

Mary grabbed his hand and held it tightly. "No such thing Tom. Uncle Billy will sort something out, just you see."

Tom nodded his head in agreement. If anyone could find a solution to the problem Uncle Billy would do it. "Could you read me a story, mum?"

"Ok Tom, how about Treasure Island. We started to read it last week. I'll just read you a couple of chapters."

"Wow yes, that's a great adventure!" he exclaimed. He snuggled down in his bed and fell fast asleep before Mary could finish the second chapter.

The next morning Tom woke to his mother's shout from the kitchen. He rubbed his eyes, clambered out of bed, and drew the curtains back. The early morning sun peeped over the roof of the barn. The rain had gone and not a cloud was visible in a pale blue sky.

Tom struggled into his school uniform. The tie was a problem. No matter how much he tried when looking through the mirror, he could not tie a decent knot. Admitting defeat, he hurtled down the stairs into the kitchen, avoiding the banister rail, to ask his mother to complete the task.

His breakfast sat on the kitchen table waiting for him. It consisted of a bowl of cornflakes, a slice of warm buttered toast and a glass of fresh orange juice.

"Good morning mum," Tom chirped, as he sat and dug his spoon into the jar of syrup, drizzling a large portion onto the cornflakes, followed by a serving of fresh farm milk poured from a glass bottle.

"Where's Uncle Billy and Auntie Nellie?" he asked between mouthfuls of cornflakes.

Mary pulled out a chair and sat down next to him. "Well, Uncle Billy had breakfast early and drove down into Middlebrook for a meeting with the bank manager and Auntie Nellie is upstairs making the bed."

"Has the tramp gone now mum?" he asked.

"Yes, he has Tom. He said goodbye to Uncle Billy and wandered off down the lane. Thank goodness the sun is shining today. I'm sure he will find work somewhere else," then patting his shoulder briefly she stood up and continued. "Now stop all this chattering and finish your breakfast or you will never be a big lad. Then get yourself off to school and DO NOT TALK TO ANY STRANGERS," she added with emphasis.

Tom was only a small boy for his age, but he had a strong, lean body. A shock of black hair topped his head and freckles covered his cheeks. He had a gentle and understanding nature which helped him make friends easily. He popped his school shoes on, pulled up his socks, picked up his satchel and opened the door, crossing the farmyard to the gate that led to the lane.

The country lane meandered through the saturated fields until it finally joined the main road. To the left lay the town of Middlebrook. Tom turned right and headed towards the quaint village of Nether Poppet. Strolling from the farm to the village junior school usually took Tom about 20 minutes.

When he reached the market square, he stopped to watch the tradesmen setting up their stalls. A market had been held in the square on a Monday for as long as Tom could remember. He negotiated the horses and carts and the tradesmen's vans which had been parked around the perimeter of the market square whilst the traders unloaded their merchandise.

He eventually reached School Lane where he met his school chum 'One Eyed Sid.'

Sidney had carried the nickname, given to him by his classmates, from his first day at school. The right lens in his glasses had been blanked off with a white sticking plaster.

Unfortunately for Sidney, he had been born with a lazy right eye. The doctors had told his mother that if Sidney did not use his right eye, then the impediment would eventually correct itself. Hence the white plaster remains in its designated position.

Sidney had taken his nickname on board and quite liked the sound of it. He told Tom in secret that the name made him feel like a famous gangster he had seen in a film at his local cinema.

"Hi One Eye," said Tom. "Have you had a good weekend?"

"Not bad," replied One Eye. "We were all supposed to go to the Harvest Fair on Saturday, but it was cancelled because of the bad weather. So," he said with a note of resignation, " I did my homework and then read one of my Just William novels."

Tom started to tell One Eye about the trouble at the farm, but One Eye continued with his story, totally oblivious to Tom's intervention. Tom knew from experience that once One Eye started a conversation, it was almost impossible to interrupt him when he was in full flow. You had to wait until One Eye slowed to take a breath and then seize the moment to tell your story.

One Eye carried on, "Then on Sunday I went to Sunday School and took a basket of fruit for the Harvest Festival. In the afternoon it was still raining, so I listened to Educating Archie on the radio and then I carried on reading my novel. Then....... "

Tom realised that the conversation had started to get a bit boring and anyway, he never listened to Educating Archie. Mainly because he could not see the sense in listening to a ventriloquist on the radio when you could not see the dummy's mouth moving.

He jumped in quickly as One Eye paused to take a breath. "My Uncle Billy has had to ask the tramp to leave because there is no work for him. The harvest crops have been ruined by the rain, so Uncle Billy has gone to meet the bank manager this morning."

"What has he done that for?" gasped One Eye.

"Well, he won't have enough money to buy food and heat the cottage through the winter. He's asking the bank manager for a loan. Things are really bad," Tom concluded.

"I'm sorry to hear that Tom," said One Eye, patting Tom on the back.

They arrived at the school gate just as the bell began to ring.

The small single story red bricked school had served the young children of the village for over one hundred years. However, the war had taken its toll on the old building. Little maintenance had been carried out and now the dark green paint on the iron framed windows and gutters had started to fade away. The ornamental black iron railings which originally sat on top of the playground wall had been cut down and taken away to help the war effort. The unheated brick toilet block stood alone in the playground. In winter every child in the school dreaded having to pay it a visit. The trick was to drink as little as possible during the day, keep your legs crossed and only go when it was really, really necessary.

The boys were in their final year at the junior school. Next year they would travel to the high school in Middlebrook. Neither of them looked forward to that experience.

The two boys stood at the back of the line in the playground as they were the eldest in the class. As they entered the classroom, Mr Scroggett, their teacher, slowly rose from his desk to greet them.

He was a nasty little man with small beady eyes and a hooked nose. "Good morning, you horrible little maggots."

"Good morning Mr Scroggett," they all chanted in unison.

"Right then. Let's see if I can try to drive the principles of decimalisation into those pea sized brains. Sit down!" he shouted.

The desks were lined up in pairs facing the front of the classroom. A narrow passage ran between each row. Tom sat next to One Eye on the front row. He could never understand why maths should be the first lesson on a Monday morning. It always put a dark cloud over his weekend thinking about it.

Tom decided that Mr Honeybunch, the headmaster, who prepared the curriculum for the school, must have a really cruel streak in his body.

Tom lifted the lid on his desk and picked up his pen and pencil, together with his maths exercise book. Before closing the desk lid, he glanced at the comments scratched in the timber from previous pupils. When he read them it always made him chuckle to himself.

'I died here of boredom. RIP'

'Old scroggy is a moggy'

'Honeybunch is the devil in disguise'

Mr Scroggett then spent the next twenty minutes standing with his back to the class, scribbling sums on the blackboard. Decimals were not Tom's favourite subject. He had to really concentrate to solve the sums written on the blackboard.

Mr Scroggett completed his task and walked to the back of the classroom. He had a bad habit of quietly strolling up the passages between the desks and peering over the pupil's shoulder. If he noticed that the pupil had made an error, he would cuff the back of their head with the flat of his hand.

Tom glanced nervously over his shoulder to see if he was coming up behind him. Fortunately, Mr Scroggett glided past him to the front of the class and seated himself at his desk. Tom worked his way through the sums and was relieved to hear the break time bell ringing. In the playground he joined One Eye and his other two friends, Jack and Harry.

The boys had been good mates since they met at school. Their parents were all part of the farming community and from being young, the boys had been involved in the various fetes and shows arranged by the farmers in the local area.

Tom had learnt in his first year at school which pupils in his class were trouble. In particular, he kept his distance from a girl named Carol Black, who had very long fingernails. If you crossed her you would be likely to end up with five parallel lines of blood red scratches across your cheek!

Arthur Creeper was also a nasty piece of work. He would take his bubble gum out of his mouth just before you were about to sit down and place it on your chair. The result was drastic.

When Tom was in year one, the children in his class were invited by Miss Jones, the teacher, to bring in their favourite toy to play with in the last hour of the school day.

Tom had brought his new green tractor to school. It had been given to him by Uncle Billy as a Christmas present. He had felt extremely proud when he walked into the classroom, carrying the tractor in its box. The children had gathered round him at lunch time eager to see the tractor. His three friends thought it was amazing and even the girls in the class had been quite impressed. However, Freddie Bumper, overcome with jealousy, had made a sarcastic comment about Tom always having the best things, because his uncle spoiled him.

Tom had ignored him, but there were to be repercussions. That day, one hour before the children were to go home, Miss Jones had allowed them to play with the toys they had brought to school. Tom had lifted his desk lid up and took out the tractor in its box. Just then, a loud scream had come from the back of the classroom. Freddie Bumper, frantically jumping up and down, had just discovered that the little red motor car which he had brought to school had disappeared. Miss Jones, on searching Freddie's desk, found that it was nowhere to be seen. Freddie had then looked across at Tom and pointed his finger at him accusing him of pinching his motor car.

Tom had been dumbfounded and could not speak. Miss Jones had asked him to empty his desk. There, hidden below his exercise books sat the little red motor car. There had been a gasp from all the children. Tom had protested his innocence to Miss Jones, but she would not listen and had sent him immediately to Mr Honeybunch's office.

Sitting in the corridor waiting to be called into the office he had tried to make sense of the situation. Why was the red car found in his desk? Who could have put it there? Then suddenly it had come to him in a flash. He'd remembered the comments Freddie Bumper made about him when he showed his tractor to the class. So, Freddie must have hidden the car in his desk during the lunch break. But how could he prove his innocence? Nobody had seen Freddie place the car in his desk and certainly Mr. Honeybunch would not believe his story.

After what had seemed an eternity, he had been called into the office. Mr Honeybunch standing in front of his desk had glared at Tom. He was a giant of a man, towering over Tom. When he leaned on his desk it creaked and groaned in protest. He always wore a grey suit, the jacket so tight that the buttons strained to burst out of the buttonholes. His large bald head resembled a watermelon with a black moustache and brown beady eyes. He'd asked Tom how the car came to be in the desk, after Tom had explained why he had been sent to him.

Tom had decided there and then that he would have to take his punishment and had just said that he'd no idea how the car had found its way into his desk. Mr Honeybunch was a tyrant and enjoyed the opportunity to thrash young children. He'd walked to his desk, took a cane from the drawer and commanded Tom to bend over. Thereupon, he'd brought the cane down three times onto the back of Tom's legs. The experience had brought tears to Tom's eyes. From that day, he'd decided never to go anywhere near Freddie Bumper ever again.

After the morning break, Mr Scroggett continued with a geography lesson on the British Isles. He wrote a list of all the cities in Britain on the blackboard. He then instructed the class to draw a map of the British Isles in their exercise books and locate all the cities on the map. Tom enjoyed geography and had no problem in carrying out the task. Seated next to him, One Eye was finding difficulty in even drawing the map, let alone locating the cities on it.

Under the watchful eyes of Mr Scroggett, it was impossible for Tom to give his friend any assistance. Fortunately, whilst Tom tried to slide his exercise book across to his friend, the school secretary wandered into the classroom and whispered something to Mr Scroggett, who then nodded and suddenly stood up following the secretary out of the classroom.

Tom could hear voices in the corridor outside the classroom. He quickly snatched One Eye's exercise book off his desk and sketched the map on a blank page, returning it just as Mr Scroggett entered the classroom. One Eye turned to Tom and gave him a nod and a wink with his good eye.

Mr Scroggett sat at his desk for the rest of the lesson, breaking a lifetime habit of patrolling the classroom. He just sat and stared into space, oblivious to his surroundings. His thoughts were broken by the sound of the lunchtime bell. The class slowly filed out of the classroom, but Mr Scroggett remained seated at his desk, head in his hands.

Tom and his friends met in the refectory for lunch. They all sat at the same table whilst they ate their hot meal.

"What was all that about then?" asked Jack. Tom shrugged his shoulders; he'd just started to say something when from the corner of his eye he glimpsed Arthur Creeper sidling up towards them.

"Guess what, you lot. The cook told my mum that she has just heard a news flash on the radio. It seems that the bank in Middlebrook has been attacked by a gang of robbers. They have stolen loads and loads of money!" he exclaimed.

Before the boys were able to question Arthur, he had drifted off to spread the news. He obviously felt very important. After all his mum worked in the kitchen and so Arthur would have been the first pupil to hear about the deadly deed.

"That's why Old Scroggy looked as though he had seen a ghost," said One Eye. "His wife is a clerk at the bank."

"You have to be joking!" exclaimed Harry. "No one, but no one would marry Old Scroggy."

"Well, we all have our cross to bear," One Eye concluded.

Tom sat in silence during the conversation. It had crossed his mind that Uncle Billy might have been in the bank when the raid took place. He decided to go straight home after school. He had intended to play with Jack and Harry at their farm, but he was anxious to find out if Uncle Billy had arrived home safely.

When they returned to the classroom Mr Scroggett was nowhere to be seen. The class four teacher, Miss Denney, sat at his desk. "I'm sorry children, but Mr Scroggett has been called away and will not be back again today," she informed the class. "I will take lessons this afternoon. We will start with English until break and then you can read until school finishes."

Tom breathed a sigh of relief. He did not want any stress this afternoon after hearing the bad news and anyway he enjoyed English and reading.

Miss Denney was a jolly decent person and Tom had taken a liking to her during his time spent in her class. The afternoon past so quickly, Tom was quite surprised when he heard the school bell ring at home time.

Tom walked quickly up School Lane with his friends and explained to them that he wanted to get home as soon as possible to see his Uncle Billy. They parted company at the Market Square and Tom broke into a run. As he tried to negotiate past a market trader carrying boxes to his van he crashed into Mr Davies, his neighbour.

"Steady on lad!" shouted Mr Davies, grabbing Tom's arm as they both fell to the ground. The market trader helped Mr Davies to his feet and Tom scrambled up dusting down his school uniform. Mr Davies seemed a bit shaky, so Tom held his arm and apologised to him and told him the news about the bank robbery.

"Well, you have no need to worry yourself, young Tom. I have just left your Uncle Billy at the farm. I believe that unfortunately, he has been unable to get the loan from the bank manager." Tom was devastated. He said his goodbyes to Mr Davies and trudged off across the market square in a daze.

CHAPTER 3: THE TRAMPS TALE

'I CANNOT RECALL ANY DETAILS OF MY LIFE BEFORE THAT FATEFUL DAY.

IT IS AS IF MY MEMORY HAS BEEN WIPED COMPLETELY AWAY, LIKE THE WRITING SCRAWLED ON THE SAND WASHED AWAY BY THE INCOMING SEA.

I AM AN OLDER MAN NOW, BUT I AM STILL PLAGUED BY A RECURRING DREAM THAT HAUNTS ME DAY AND NIGHT.

I GO TO SLEEP TRYING TO REMEMBER THE PAST AND I WAKE UP IN A COLD SWEAT.

THIS IS MY DREAM.....

I AM STANDING IN THE MIDDLE OF A SNOW-COVERED FIELD ON A CRISP SUNNY MORNING.

ALL AROUND ME BODIES LIE SCATTERED FACE DOWN IN THE SNOW.

THE BARE, BLACKENED TREES STAND LIKE SILENT SENTINELS, THEIR BRANCHES REACHING UP IN DESPAIR TO THE HEAVENS.

THE AIR AROUND ME IS FILLED WITH THE SOUND OF THUNDER. IT FEELS LIKE MY EARDRUMS ARE GOING TO BURST.

FROM OUT OF NOWHERE, A GREAT BALL OF FIRE ROLLS ACROSS THE FIELD GATHERING MOMENTUM AND GETTING LARGER AS IT APPROACHES ME.

IT LEAVES A BLACKENED PATH IN THE MELTED SNOW.

I TURN AND START TO RUN FOR MY LIFE... MY BOOTS FEEL LIKE LEAD AS I TRUDGE THROUGH THE DEEP LAYER OF SOFT SNOW.

I CAN FEEL THE INTENSE HEAT ON THE BACK OF MY HEAD AS THE BALL OF FIRE COMES CLOSER.

MY UNIFORM BEGINS TO SMOULDER, THE HAIR ON MY HEAD STARTS TO CRACKLE.

I KNOW NOW THAT THERE IS NO ESCAPE FROM THE INFERNO THAT WILL ENVELOP ME.

I STUMBLE AND FALL FACE DOWN INTO THE SOFT, COOL SNOW AND WAIT FOR THE END.

MY BODY BURNS AND THE FLESH ON THE BACK OF MY HANDS BEGINS TO CRAWL.

SILENCE SURROUNDS ME NOW.

I AM AT PEACE..........

Macky's thoughts are interrupted by a continual tapping sound. He places his pencil down on his notepad and slowly turns his head, glancing through the café window to see Tom standing outside.

Macky saluted Tom and then gestured to him.

Tom hesitated, then pushed the door slowly open to the café. The warmth from inside Bettys Café hit his face as he entered.

The café was crowded with locals of all ages, chattering away in low voices as they swopped stories about the local scandals. Each trying to outdo the other on the information that they had gleaned from unknown sources.

Tom noticed the only vacant chair in the café and sat down facing Macky.

This meeting would be the first time Tom had been so close to Macky since he started work at the farm. Tom didn't even know his name, because, as far as he knew, everyone calls him 'the tramp'. "Hello young Tom, have you had a good day at school?" asked Macky.

"Not bad for a Monday sir," Tom replied. He studied Macky with interest. He was shocked to see that the back of his hands had been badly burnt and what he could see of his face appeared to be covered in jagged scars.

"Skin grafts Tom. Lots of them," said Macky, answering Tom's thoughts.

"Crickey!" exclaimed Tom. "How awful. Who did that to you sir?" he stammered.

"If only I knew Tom," he replied, "tell you what Tom, why don't you call me Macky. Everyone else that I know calls me Macky for some unknown reason."

Tom noticed the writing pad on the table.

"Are you writing a story about your adventures Macky?"

"Well not quite Tom. You see I have completely lost my memory. All I can remember is waking up in a hospital bed wrapped in bandages from head to foot, looking like an Egyptian mummy."

Tom gasped and Macky continued, "so, now I have decided to write down all the details that I can remember about a terrible dream, or should I say nightmare, that I keep having. This may help to jog my memory and eventually I hope I will be able to remember what really happened to me and who I am."

"But when you woke up in the hospital bed did the doctors not tell you what happened?" Tom asked.

"Not really Tom. They said that a troop of British soldiers found me in a field in Northern France, lying face down in the deep snow, completely unconscious, my uniform burnt to shreds. They wrapped me in a trench coat, put me on a stretcher and carried me to a field hospital."

"What on earth were you doing in France Macky?" interjected Tom.

"Well, I reckon that I must have been fighting in the war against the German forces, but I have no idea how I got there. You see it was February 1944 when I ended up in the hospital in England and the war didn't finish until 1945."

"But how long did you have to stay in the hospital?" Tom asked.

"A very long time Tom, because I had suffered terrible burns to my face and hands. The doctors had to give me many skin grafts and then I had to convalesce for months."

Tom sat in silence considering the thought of having to have the skin taken from one part of your body and grafted onto the parts that had been burnt away, ugh.

He had a sudden thought, "But surely, if you were in the army you would have identification papers that would tell the doctors who you were and in which regiment you were serving?" "Well Tom, that's the problem. You must understand that my uniform was so badly burnt that any papers that I carried had been destroyed. Even the identification disc that had been on a chain around my neck had disappeared."

"So, what did you do when you eventually left the hospital?" queried Tom.

"Soldiers coming home from the war were given what they call demob suits together with two shirts, a tie, shoes and a raincoat. I decided to sell the suit, raincoat and shoes on the black market and buy some corduroy trousers and a jacket. I already had the trench coat that they wrapped me up in when they found me in France. I finally bought a pair of strong, black leather boots, because I was going to be doing a lot of walking."

"Why didn't you just go and get a job when you left the hospital, Macky?" Tom asked.

Macky paused for a moment to gather his thoughts. "You have to remember Tom that thousands of soldiers were returning to England at the end of the war. Jobs were very difficult to come by because the bombing had destroyed factories and businesses. What chance did I have when I couldn't even remember what I did before the beginning of the war?"

"So, I decided to hit the road and look for manual work at the various farms scattered about the countryside. I have been travelling now for seven years, sleeping in barns during the winter and under hedges in summertime."

"Wow!" exclaimed Tom, "what a great adventure."

"Not really Tom," replied Macky, with a sigh, "it's great when the sun is shining, but in winter it is damn cold and wet. I eventually had to invest in a sleeping bag and a small tent to keep me warm."

"Well, I hope that writing down your dreams brings your memory back, Macky."

"We will see laddie. Now, shouldn't you be making tracks for home? Your mum will be getting worried. I'll walk with you part of the way if you don't mind Tom. I'm not doing anything else," he chuckled.

CHAPTER 4: THE ROBBERS

Tom and Macky strolled up the country lane towards the farmhouse. It was so quiet, but for the birds singing and the occasional background drone of a vehicle on the main road to Middlebrook.

The hedgerows were full of blackberries, ready for picking and boiling, eventually ending up in a tasty pie. The ditches on each side of the lane had filled to the top with muddy flood water, draining from the fields.

From the main road, the lane meandered through the surrounding fields and terminated at the farmyard gate. The only traffic to use the lane would usually be the postman's van, Uncle Billy's old Land Rover and the rusty old blue farm tractor, which left mounds of dark brown mud splattered in its tracks.

So, when the pair were about halfway up the lane, Tom was surprised to see a large black motor car, parked with two wheels on the grass verge in front of a gate to the fields.

Tom and Macky stopped in their tracks when they spotted the car. The front of the car pointed in their direction, as if it had come from the farmhouse. Tell-tale wisps of exhaust fumes drifted from the rear of the car.

"That's very strange," muttered Tom as they approached the black car.

"Engine's running," Macky commented.

"But where's the occupants?" Tom queried.

They both looked up and down the lane. Not a person in sight.

When they reached the car, Macky peered through the passenger door window.

"The car keys are dangling from the ignition switch Tom."

Tom turned the shiny chrome door handle. The door swung slowly open.

He stuck his head into the interior. "Wow, classy car. It's got a walnut dashboard, cream leather seats and plush brown carpet."

"Who the heck would leave a car like this in the lane with the doors open and the engine running. Unbelievable!" Macky exclaimed.

"Beats me," replied Tom, as he glanced up and then down the lane to see if he could see the driver. Then he continued, "perhaps there's a dead body in the boot and the murderer has abandoned the car."

Macky stood and scratched his beard. "Well, there's only one way to find out if there is Tom."

With that, he strolled to the rear of the black car and cautiously turned the handle on the boot lid. As the boot lid swung upwards, they both suddenly stepped back in amazement.

The boot was stuffed with brown canvas sacks brimming over with bank notes. "Oh, my goodness!" exclaimed Macky. "I don't like this one bit. We have to get this car to the police station, Tom and pronto!"

"I don't understand?" said Tom.

"My bet is that this jolly lolly is from the bank raid in town and we are sitting on one hot potato," Macky concluded.

"But why would the robbers leave the car here?" said Tom in exasperation.

"I can't answer that, Tom, but we have to go now laddie."

Tom was hesitant. "Do you think you could drive the car Macky?"

Macky considered the situation whilst scratching his beard again.

"Must be a habit," Tom thought to himself.

"Don't know Tom, can't remember. Let's give it a go then we will find out," he chortled.

Macky slung his knapsack onto the back seat and jumped into the driver's seat. Tossing his satchel onto the back seat, Tom slid in next to him, feeling slightly nervous.

With the engine already running, it was just a matter of pressing the clutch pedal down, slipping the car into gear and releasing the handbrake.

Tom recited the procedure to Macky. He had travelled in Uncle Billy's Land Rover many times and had watched his Uncle start it up.

The large black car lurched forward when Macky depressed the accelerator pedal and quickly gathered speed as it moved down the lane. "By jove, I think I've got it laddie," shouted Macky. Suddenly, they heard a very loud bang followed by the sound of the car's rear window shattering into a thousand pieces.

"Crickey," exclaimed Tom. "What's going on?"

Macky glanced through the rear-view mirror and was astounded to see a large plump man staggering from the field behind them, pulling his trousers up from around his ankles with one hand whilst firing a revolver at them with the other hand.

The car started to swerve from side to side as Macky wrestled with the steering wheel trying to regain control.

A second bullet from the revolver had pierced the tyre at the rear, causing it to rupture.

Macky struggled to keep the car on the road. Unwittingly he had kept his foot on the accelerator pedal and now they were speeding towards a sharp bend on the lane.

"Slow down Macky!" screamed Tom. But it was too late now. The car careered off the lane like a missile, ploughing nose first into the ditch and coming to a sudden halt in the bushes. The engine had stalled, a deathly silence now hung over the wrecked car.

The bonnet from the black car had been torn from its fixings and lay in the field beyond the hedge. A steady plume of steam rose from the ruptured radiator in the engine compartment.

Macky had been propelled forward with such ferocity that his head had hit the windscreen and now he lay slumped across the steering wheel. Fortunately for Tom, with being so small, he had slid off the passenger seat, ending up in the footwell below the dashboard.

The car swung at a crazy angle with its rear wheels lifted clear of the road surface and its front end firmly planted in the ditch and surrounding hedge. The boot lid had sprung open under the impact and bank notes were slowly drifting away in the evening breeze.

The large plump man lumbered up to the car waving his revolver in the air and shouting obscenities.

Whilst he was jumping up and down attempting in vain to reach the handle on the boot lid, a small green van came speeding up the lane and screeched to a halt near the black car.

A thin, weasel faced man, wearing blue overalls and a black flat cap climbed out of the van and approached the plump man. "What the hell yer doin Bert? I only left yer for 15 minutes after we did the robbery to pick up the van and drive it here. Yer, were supposed to be waiting for me so we can move the money from the car to the van."

Bert stood in his crumpled brown pinstripe suit, his shiny black shoes covered in mud and his revolver hanging down by his side.

"I know them were the arrangements Sid, but I were having a quiet moment behind the bushes when these two cretins pinched me car."

"Just a minute Bert, I think I've missed somefin here. What two cretins are yer talking about?"

Bert pointed nervously to the front of the black car.

Sid walked up to the passenger door and standing on his tiptoes looked through the window. "I don't believe it. Are they dead? They must be dead. What are we goin to do with two dead bodies? A fine mess yer've got us into now Bert," ranted Sid.

Sid's attention was drawn to a bank note floating above his head, "What yer done with the money Bert. Feeding the birds with crisp banknotes then?" he shouted, his face getting redder and redder as saliva ran down from the corner of his mouth.

"That were what I were going to tell yer next," stuttered Bert, "the blinking boot lid flew open when the car crashed and I couldn't reach the handle to close it," he replied with little conviction in his voice.

Sid's eyes glazed over as he looked up to heaven and muttered a short prayer under his breath. "Tell me this then, wooden head!" he screamed. "Why do yer want to close the rotten boot lid when we can't drive this wreck of a car away and we are supposed to be moving the cash from it to the blinking van!"

"Oh yea, I forgot about that in the panic Sid, sorry," he muttered.

"Quick, give us a hand," said Sid, "bend down and give me a piggyback."

"I don't think this is the time to play party games Sid," replied Bert.

"No, you idiot, with me on yer shoulders I can get in the boot and hand the sacks of money down to yer."

Bert scratched the top of his head. "OK, if yer say so Sid."

Sid carefully climbed up onto Bert's back then up to his shoulders.

Bert staggered upright and Sid wriggled into the open boot.

The car gently rocked when Sid slid into the boot. He quickly fastened the open sacks to prevent any more bank notes escaping, then slowly handed each sack down to Bert. "Right then. We put the sacks in the van and then collect as many of the notes scattered on the lane," instructed Sid.

Then Sid had a sudden thought, "we can then figure out how to dispose of the dead bodies," he said.

"Why not just leave em in the car Sid?"

"Great idea Bert. So, we will not only be bank robbers, but murderers as well. How long do yer think we'll be put in the slammer if they ever catch us then? They won't believe it were just an accident."

Bert slowly nodded his head, not quite understanding the logic behind Sid's argument. "Ok Sid. Why don't we just bury em so nobody will ever find the bodies."

They both gave a high five, picked up the sacks and walked towards the van.

BERT WAVING HIS REVOLVER.

CHAPTER 5: THE BLACK CAR

Tom sat crouched in the footwell not daring to move a muscle. His left ankle throbbed like mad. His foot had twisted under the weight of his body when he had catapulted off his seat and landed on the floor below the car dashboard. A swelling started to appear on his right elbow which, unfortunately, had struck the car's gear lever when he'd thrust his arm out to prevent his head colliding with the dashboard.

Macky lay slumped over the steering wheel, completely still, his head pressed against the car's shattered windscreen. A trickle of blood ran slowly down his cheek from a deep gash on his forehead. His broken sunglasses had disappeared into the footwell.

Tom could hear the voices of the men, feeling the car move as they lifted the sacks from its boot. As silence fell, he slowly tried to wriggle out of the footwell. The pain from his injured ankle prevented him pushing his body into an upright position. Lying on his front across the seat, he stretched his arm across to Macky and tried to shake him in the hope that he was still alive.

Macky grunted and muttered under his breath. He forced himself off the steering wheel and sat bolt upright in the car seat. Tom was just about to whisper to Macky when he heard a sharp tapping sound on the window behind him.

With great effort he turned his head and his gaze fell upon a frightening sight. A pale-yellow, pock marked face with dark brown, beady eyes set above a sharp hooked nose and cruel, thin twisted lips stared down at him.

Sid, the weasel grasped the door handle and pulled it open.

Tom screamed at the top of his voice.

Macky threw his arms into the air and started waving them wildly about while shouting like a man insane, "Everybody out now!! We've suffered a direct hit and are in danger of being enveloped in fire." Sid stopped in his tracks and Tom looked on in fear as Macky threw his body at the car door to try and escape, "quickly sergeant, release the turret bolts and evacuate the tank as quickly as possible. It's every man for himself now!" he ranted.

In an uncontrollable frenzy he clambered over into the back seat, snatched up his knapsack, smashed the car window with his elbow and started to climb out of the car.

"Macky, Macky what are you doing?" shouted Tom, as Macky's feet disappeared from his view.

Macky fell from the car and plunged headfirst into the ditch, clinging to his beloved knapsack.

Sid and Bert ran around the back of the car to the ditch as Macky slowly crawled out of the ditch, muddy water dripping from his trench coat and green slime plastered across his face.

Bert quickly drew his revolver and pointed it at Macky. "No don't," said Sid as he placed his hand over the revolver and pushed it down, "get the kid, shove him in the back of the van and tie him up," Sid commanded.

Bert started to pull Tom from the car. He screamed in pain as Bert tried to march him back to the car. "My ankle is killing me. I can't walk." Tom sobbed.

"Ok, yer snivelling little wretch, then I'll just drag yer to the van," Bert shouted. Whereupon Bert snatched Tom's collar and started to do just that.

Sid grabbed Macky's coat and pulled him from the ditch. Macky lay face down muttering incoherently. "Right then mate," said Sid, "now that both yer and the kid have seen our faces, we can't leave yer here, can we?"

Bert strolled back carrying a length of rope. "When can we bury 'em, Sid?" he said eagerly. Sid turned to Bert and muttered a short prayer to himself. "Well Bert, seeing as they're not dead yet, don't yer think it would be kind of stupid to try and bury em?"

"Er, well, ok Sid," he remarked, "maybe another time. Do we tie this bloke up then?"

Sid nodded in resignation. They set about their task with little resistance from Macky, who in the meantime had drifted into a trance. They dragged him back along the lane to the rear of the van. The strap of Macky's knapsack had caught around his ankle and trailed along behind him.

Before loading him into the van, Sid stretched over and took a large metal can out of the van. "Right then Bert, soak the inside of the car with petrol from the can and then set fire to it."

Bert looked at him in amazement. "We destroy all the fingerprints and any trace of these two cretins. Job well done," Sid chirped, standing with his arms folded and a smug look on his face.

Bert hesitated, then slowly walked towards the car carrying the can of petrol.

He opened the front car doors and poured a quantity of petrol onto the seats. He looked up at the open boot. His final act was to throw the can with the remaining contents into the boot.

Unfortunately for Bert, his aim was not entirely accurate. The can struck the side of the open boot lid, flipped round, turned upside down and poured its remaining contents onto poor Bert, who stood with an open mouth looking up at the cascading liquid. "Crikey," spluttered Bert as the petrol sprayed his face and ran down his neck, soaking his clothes.

"For crying out loud, can't yer do anything right!" screamed Sid.

Bert started rooting in his trouser pocket for a box of matches. "DO NOT, I SAY, DO NOT STRIKE A MATCH!!" Sid shouted in panic, as he ran towards Bert, lunging for the box of matches in Bert's hand and knocking him off his feet.

The two men rolled about in the dirt of the lane, screaming at each other. Sid eventually managed to sit astride Bert, his face contorted with rage. "What do yer think yer doin yer idiot. We could have been blown to kingdom come!" he screamed. After a short pause he added. "Heck, yer don't half stink!"

Bert lay prostrate under Sid, gasping for breath. "Can...I...get..up...now, Sid?" he stammered.

Sid stood up, pulling Bert to his feet. "Right then Bert. Yer goin to take yer clothes off."

"What!" shrieked Bert, "In full daylight!"

"Well yer not travelling in the van stinking of petrol."

Bert thought for a moment. "Ok then, but can I leave me underpants and vest on?"

"Of course yer can Bert. In fact, there's a spare pair of overalls in the van. Yer can put em on."

Bert cautiously removed his jacket and shirt. He slowly dropped his trousers, exposing bright yellow boxer shorts with large red polka dots adorning them. Sid sniggered to himself.

"Well yer do look a sight for sore eyes Bert. Now go and wash yer face and hair in the dyke to get rid of the petrol."

Bert staggered to the dyke. Slowly kneeling down, he stuck his head into the muddy water. Within seconds of submerging his head, he jumped up spluttering and shouting. A coating of slimy water and weeds clung to his head.

"Go back to the van and put on the overalls, then shove the geezer in the back of the van with the kid," Sid instructed. "I'll set fire to the car."

Bert stomped back to the van, uttering curses under his breath.

Sid strolled around the car inspecting Bert's handywork.

Rather than just throw a lit match into the car he decided to use Bert's clothes, which now lay on the lane, as a taper. He carefully picked each item up with two fingers and positioned them in a continuous line which led to the open car door.

Standing way back from the car, he struck a match and dropped it onto Bert's petrol-soaked jacket. It instantly caught fire, the flame jumping from the jacket to the shirt and finally to the trousers.

The instant it reached the car there was a terrific whooshing sound as the interior caught fire and enveloped the vehicle in flames. The heat from the back draught hit Sid in the face taking his breath away. He turned and ran back to the van as fast as his legs could carry him.

Bert, now dressed in blue overalls, had managed to drag Macky into the van. Throwing his knapsack in behind him and leaving the back doors open he turned in horror to watch the car disappear in a sea of flames.

Sid raced up the lane shouting for Bert to close the van doors and get into the passenger seat.

Bert slammed the doors closed and jumped into the van. Sid started the engine and executed a well-judged three point turn on the narrow lane.

Unknown to the two men, the car's petrol tank still contained half a tank of fuel. As Sid revved up the engine and casually set off down the lane, a tremendous explosion was followed instantly by an enormous fireball that erupted and shot up towards the heavens from the burning car behind them.

Macky, now lying on his back in the van, still semiconscious, suddenly went ballistic as he watched the fireball through the van's rear window. "There's no escape. We are all doomed!" he screamed at the top of his voice as the flames from the fireball reflected in his glazed eyes. Sid glanced at the van's wing mirror. "Bert. For god's sake, I thought I told yer to set it on fire, NOT blow it to smithereens!" He laughed out loud as he pressed the accelerator hard down to the floor and the little green van sped off down the lane.

CHAPTER 6: THE FIRE BRIGADE TO THE RESCUE

Uncle Billy paced up and down, his stockinged feet sliding silently across the smooth polished flagstones on the kitchen floor. "For goodness sake Billy!" exclaimed his wife, "you're going to wear those flags out before you're finished."

Uncle Billy suddenly halted and turned to face his wife and Mary seated at the kitchen table. "Young Tom has never been late home from school. Something's gone wrong, Nellie."

"Telephone One Eye, he's Tom's best friend. Perhaps he went back with him to play at his farm. He does that sometimes," Nellie suggested.

"Never done that before without telling us," Mary replied anxiously, screwing a handkerchief up in her hands.

Uncle Billy shuffled off into the hall to call One Eyes's parents. As he approached the telephone, it suddenly began to ring. Uncle Billy grabbed the receiver, quickly lifting it up to his ear. "Hello Billy," a short pause, "I'm sorry to hear about the trouble at the bank. I hope you are OK."

It took Uncle Billy a moment to recognise the voice of his neighbour, Mr Davies. "Oh, yes John. I'm fine. The robbery happened after I left the bank, but as you know, I wasn't able to get the loan from the bank manager."

"Yes, I was sorry to hear that Billy. If you need any help at the farm don't hesitate to contact me."

"I've got bigger worries than that now John. Young Tom hasn't come home from school and we are all worried sick."

"Hang on a minute Billy," said Mr Davies, "I bumped into Tom in the Market Square on his way from school. When he left me, he popped into Bettys Café. I think he saw the tramp who worked at your farm."

"Well where the devil is he then?" said Uncle Billy anxiously.

"You had better call the police Billy and tell them Tom has gone missing. LAST SEEN TALKING TO THE TRAMP," he emphasised.

Uncle Billy said his goodbyes and walked slowly back into the kitchen, deep in thought, as he sat down at the kitchen table.

"Who was that?" asked Mary.

"Mr. Davies dear. He saw Tom at Betty's Café in the Market Square talking to the tramp. I'm going to call the police and_____."

Uncle Billy's words were drowned out by the sound of an enormous explosion which rattled the tiles on the roof of the farmhouse.

"What the hell was that!" exclaimed Auntie Nellie, dropping her knitting needles.

All three jumped up together and ran out of the farmhouse fearing that the building was about to collapse. They stopped suddenly in the farmyard gazing in awe across the meadows. For there, in the distance, rose a large black plume of smoke, intermingled with vivid red and yellow flames soaring high into the sky.

Uncle Billy turned to face Aunty Nellie. "Call the police Nellie. Tell them about Tom. Mary and I are going to see what on earth has happened."

Mary and Uncle Billy ran down the country lane towards the flames. After what seemed an eternity, they reached a bend in the lane. They could smell the stench of petrol hanging in the still air. Uncle Billy grabbed Mary's hand. "We must be very cautious now Mary. There may still be more explosions."

As they walked slowly hand in hand around the bend, the heat from the burning car punched them in the face.

"Crickey," gasped Mary, holding one hand in front of her face to shield her from the searing heat. They stood side by side in silence watching the flames leaping up from the burning car, unable to approach any closer.

"Nobody could survive that inferno," muttered Uncle Billy.

In the distance they could hear the bells of emergency vehicles approaching.

CHAPTER 7: THE RIDE IN THE GREEN VAN

Tom's ankle and elbow were aching like mad. The ribbed metal floor of the van dug into his back as the van bounced along the rough surface of the lane.

Macky lay completely subdued on his back, muttering each time the van hit a bump on the lane.

Tom managed to push himself up into a sitting position, now leaning with his back resting on the side panel of the van. From his new position he could look through the small windows in the rear doors of the van. Hedgerows and trees were flashing past them as the van sped down the lane.

Suddenly, Sid slammed on the brakes and the van came to an abrupt stop. Tom was thrown backwards, unable to stop himself, the rope binding his wrists cutting into his skin. His head banged against the solid timber panel at the front of the van, which separated them from the driver's cab. He slowly slid down to the floor in a daze.

Lying on the floor of the van with his head pressed up against the timber panel, Tom could just make out the raised voices of the men in the cab, but he was unable to hear clearly why they were arguing.

An eerie silence fell in the cab and Tom thought at first that the men had abandoned the van. A sudden jolt shook Tom as the van started to go backwards, stopping again after a short distance.

Moving slowly forward it swung to the right and accelerated so fast that the sacks, Tom and Macky slid along the floor of the van crashing into the rear doors.

The impact seemed to bring Macky out of his trance. He grabbed Tom's arm, "What the heck is going on? Where are we Tom?"

"Calm down Macky," replied Tom. He then began to tell Macky about the black car in the lane and how they had ended up in the back of the van.

Macky lay in silence staring up at the roof of the van.

When Tom finished his story Macky rolled onto his side to face him.

"It's slowly coming back to me now," he said excitedly, "it wasn't a dream Tom. The fireball chasing me across a field really happened."

"I don't understand what you mean Macky," Tom replied.

"Well, when the black car burst into flames and the fireball shot into the air it brought back memories of my past life."

"Yes, I get that Macky, because when you banged your head in the car, you started rambling about escaping from a tank through its turret. Is that because it had caught fire?"

"Yes, that's right Tom. Can you remember what else I said?"

"Yes, you said, 'we have suffered a direct hit and we are all going to be consumed in fire' and then you told the sergeant to release the turret bolts and that everybody had to get out."

"That's it, Tom. I need to think really hard now and figure out why the heck I was in a tank," he suddenly noticed the sacks which contained the bank notes. "What's going on, why is all this money in the van?"

Macky had obviously forgotten the incident with the black car.

Well Macky, I think it must be the money from the bank robbery which took place at the bank in Middlebrook."

Macky stared at Tom, unable to comprehend his explanation. "OK Tom, but more to the point, where is your school satchel?"

"OH NO!" he exclaimed, "I left it on the back seat of the black car." A sudden thought struck him, "crickey, the robbers set fire to the car. All my schoolbooks have been destroyed. Gone up in smoke!"

He started to sob and Macky snuggled up to him and whispered, "Don't get upset Tom. Worse things could have happened to us. At least we are still alive and I am going to do my darndest to get us out of this mess."

The van started to bump up and down, as if it was running over very rough ground. Tom tried to push himself up into a sitting position, but the pain from his aching ankle wouldn't let him.

Macky peered out of the small window. All that he could see was a canopy of leafy branches. "I think we are travelling through a wooded area, probably on a dirt track," he concluded.

The van began to lose momentum, slowly grinding to halt. The engine died followed by complete silence.

CHAPTER 8: THE GAMEKEEPERS LODGE

Once upon a time, a palatial manor house had stood for centuries on top of a hill above the Wye Valley. Its estate stretched as far as the eye could see.

A vast woodland surrounded the manor. Tucked away in the depth of it sat a timber lodge, occupied by the gamekeeper for the estate.

At the turn of the nineteenth century the lord of the manor embarked on a major building project which would make it the grandest manor house in the country, befitting for the twentieth century.

Unfortunately, as the contractors were putting the finishing touches to the magnificent building, a disastrous tragedy occurred. A small fire started in the roof space, accidently set off by the roofer whilst he prepared the leadwork for the gutters.

The roofer stamped the fire out, or so he thought, for unfortunately he did not see that some insulating material below the rafters remained smouldering.

The contractor had left the manor house at the end of the working day assuming that the fire had been completely extinguished.

However, as the grandfather clock in the hallway struck the hour of midnight, the smouldering insulation burst into flames.

The fire spread through the roof space with such a vengeance that within the hour the whole building became consumed by a terrible inferno. The screams from the family could be heard across the valley as they tried unsuccessfully to escape the flames. All perished before help arrived. Or so it was thought.

All the bodies were recovered after the fire had died down, except for one person. The body of the lord of the manor was never found amongst the ruins.

With the house completely destroyed by the fire and no relatives available to carry on running the estate, the gamekeeper had to leave the lodge and find work elsewhere. Eventually the ruins of the manor house became covered in the deep undergrowth.

Many years later, Sid and Bert sat in the Black Cat Pub in Middlebrook eating their sausage sandwiches, washed down with a few pints of ale.

The second world war had ended two years earlier and the townsfolk of Middlebrook were still queuing outside the various food shops for basic items.

The British Government had introduced rationing in 1940 and food coupons in ration books were issued for every man, woman and child.

One way to get rationed items without coupons, usually at greatly inflated prices, was on the black market. Petty criminals traded in goods often obtained by dubious means. Sid had found a golden opportunity to make lots of money. Where the townsfolk struggled to make ends meet, Sid and Bert lived like lords. They had started selling goods on the black market.

Sid winked at Bert and pointed to an old timer sitting on his own at a corner table in the bar. "Might have a sale there Bert," he whispered.

Sid slinked across to the old timer's table and introduced himself.

They chatted about the old days and the old timer told him that in his younger days he had been employed as the gamekeeper to the manor house which had stood on the hill.

After a short time, Sid started to lose interest in the conversation until the old timer mentioned the lodge. Like a beam of light shining in Sid's small brain he suddenly realised that this could be the answer to his dreams.

A lodge, in the middle of the woods. Left unattended for half a century with only the gamekeeper knowing its whereabouts.

Sid's brain moved up a gear as he realised that the lodge would make a fantastic bolt hole to hide away after the next bank robbery that he was planning.

Sid, now showing total interest in the old timer's tale, had persuaded him to take him to see the remains of the lodge.

The little green van entered the woods to the lodge. Over the years, the track through the woods had been taken over by mother nature. With the old timer giving directions, Sid had to stop the van numerous times whilst Bert cut through the undergrowth. Eventually they reached a glade, buried deep in the woods. On the other side of the glade stood the lodge, now in a pitiful state.

The roof had collapsed. The windowpanes were smashed and the front door was nowhere to be seen. The old timer broke down in tears. What had been his home in those wonderful years spent at the manor house was now a ruin.

Sid stepped out of the van and strolled up to the lodge. Bert and the old timer sat in the van.

The old timer turned to face Bert. "You've heard the story about the lord of the manor," he whispered.

Bert stared at him, nonplussed. "No, don't think so," he replied.

"Well, the story goes, that when the manor house burnt to the ground, around about the late 19th century, all the family perished, but they never found the body of the lord of the manor."

He paused whilst Bert's tiny brain absorbed the facts. "Rumours have it that the lord of the manor escaped from the fire, saving his own skin and leaving his family to die in the flames."

"Blimey," uttered Bert, "so, where did he go then?"

The old timer looked cautiously around him, scanning the surrounding woods.

"What yer doin?" Bert said nervously.

"Well, they do say..." he paused.

"Who say?" queried Bert.

"The little people who live in the woods of course," he said, followed by a crafty wink. Bert stared at the old timer, a quizzical look across his face.

"This bloke's lost it," he thought, "obviously spent too much time in the pub."

"Ok then, what do the little people say?" Bert replied, humouring the old timer.

"The lord of the manor lives in a tree house now. At the dead of night, when it is so dark, when you can't see your hand in front of your face, he comes down and wanders the woods, looking for food whilst howling at the top of his voice. Like the wolves," pausing for effect, he continued, "do you know what he wants to eat?" Bert slowly moved his head, side to side.

"Little children! That's why they call him The Child Snatcher!"

"Crickey," murmured Bert, half believing the tale.

"So," whispered the old timer, "remember the name given to the woods?"

Bert shook his head once again.

"DEAD MANS WOOD," he said triumphantly.

At that moment, Sid opened the door to the van and Bert simultaneously pooped his pants.

Sid had considered carefully the work that would have to be done to make the lodge habitable. He realised that Bert and himself would have to spend a fair amount of money and time if they were to be able to use the lodge. But he had decided that it would be worth it at the end of the day. He had a contact who would put money into the project, provided a deal could be worked out on the next bank job.

Nobody else, but himself, Bert and the gamekeeper would ever know the location of the lodge.

Sid told Bert and the gamekeeper what he had decided to do with the lodge. He spun a fanciful tale to the gamekeeper which involved himself and Bert being keen bird watchers who wanted to use the lodge as a hide to watch the birds in secrecy.

Before driving away, he threw a glance at Bert. "Have yer seen a ghost Bert? Yer as white as a sheet," paused for a moment whilst he looked around the van, "and what's that funny smell?"

When Bert eventually plucked up the courage to tell Sid about the old timer's tale, Sid just clipped him round the ear hole and told him in no uncertain terms that he was an idiot and not to listen to a lunatic's ramblings.

So, after many months of hard labour, the lodge house looked presentable and fit to live in. A generator had been installed behind the garage to provide electricity and they had found a well in the surrounding woods to provide a water supply.

THE GAMEKEEPER'S LODGE
IN
DEAD MANS WOOD

CHAPTER 9: THE HIDEOUT

Six years had passed since that day in the woods and now Sid and Bert had returned once again. The small green van stood alone in the centre of the glade surrounded by a wall of trees towering above it.

In front of the van, on the edge of the glade sat the lodge house, with its new corrugated tin roof, now covered in a thick layer of green moss. The surrounding forest wrapped itself so tightly around the glade that it seemed impossible for the sun's rays to penetrate the thick foliage.

The van door slowly opened. Bert stepped out and strolled towards the lodge. To one side of the lodge, a timber garage lent at a precarious angle against its wall. Bert approached the garage, grabbed a handle on one of the hinged timber doors and tugged it. The door creaked and groaned in protest, until it was finally full open. Moving over to the second door, he gripped hold of the crumbling timber and, with difficulty dragged the door open. Bert turned and beckoned to Sid to drive into the garage. The green van crept towards the open doors, its rear wheels spinning on the soft, muddy surface.

With the van safely tucked away in the garage and the doors closed, Sid and Bert walked towards the lodge.

"Shall we take em out of the van now and shove em in the cellar Sid?"

"Naw, not yet, I'm gasping for a cup of char."

In the gloom of the fading day, the two men walked up to the lodge and negotiating a muddy pool, they climbed up the wooden steps to a rickety old veranda which ran across the front of the lodge. Sid pulled out a large rusty key from his pocket and poked it into a keyhole in the front door. Turning the key, he pushed the door with his shoulder.

The door needed a fresh coat of paint and the rusty hinges, a few drops of oil. Going bright red in the face and breathing heavily, Sid lashed out with his boot, kicking the door, and swearing profusely, until it slowly gave way and edged open.

The pungent smell from within the lodge took Sid's breath away. He staggered back gasping for air, bumping into Bert, impatiently waiting directly behind him. "What yer doin?" screamed Bert as he stepped back into space, his foot missing the top step on the veranda. In slow motion, with arms and hands thrashing the air in a desperate effort to find an object to grasp, he gracefully pitched backwards down the three steps and into the deep pool of dark oily mud, landing on his back and creating a very satisfactory slapping sound.

"Crickey Bert, this place stinks. What yer been doin in there?"

Completely unaware of Bert's demise, Sid turned to face him. "What the heck yer doin just lying down there when there's work to be done!" exclaimed Sid.

Bert trying with difficulty to contain his rising temper, writhed around like a maniac on steroids, as he tried unsuccessfully to free himself from the dark slimy mud. "Give us a hand bruv," gasped Bert.

Sid lifted his eyes to the heavens in desperation, then walked down the steps avoiding the pool of mud. Bert clutched his outstretched hand and Sid pulled him from the grip of the mud, not unlike a cork being ejected from a bottle of wine.

"Stay here and don't move Bert," shouted Sid, as he ran back to the garage.

Bert stood totally bewildered, the remnants of the mud sliding off his blue overalls. Sid returned pulling a length of green hose pipe from the garage. Reaching Bert, he squeezed the trigger on the gun attached to the hose pipe, sending a powerful jet of cold water at him. Within seconds and after a lot of screaming from Bert, the water blasted what remained of the mud, off his overalls, shoes and head.

"Yer a crazy man Sid. I think you enjoy inflicting pain on people," sobbed Bert, shivering in the cool air of the shady glade. Sid sniggered to himself as he turned and threw the hose pipe to the ground.

"Right then Bert, yer go in the cabin, find out what the heck is causing that foul smell and open all the windows," instructed Sid, "then, get yerself a fresh change of clothes."

Bert shuffled off into the lodge whilst Sid sat down on the veranda steps and had a smoke. After what seemed an eternity, Bert appeared at the open door, smartly dressed in a grey checked suit, powder blue shirt and shiny black leather shoes with red socks peeking out below the trousers legs.

Bert mumbled to Sid.

"What yer saying Bert? Speak up mate."

"I said, I found two rotting kippers in the cupboard under the sink."

"Well that's very nice. I wonder who the hell left em there when they were here last month, BERT!" he screamed.

"Sorry, Sorry Sid," he stammered, "I must have forgotten em when I left the lodge to case the bank in town. I had a lot on me mind yer know," he added.

"What were the last thing I told yer when I left yer in the safe house?"

"Err, make sure all the windows and doors are locked when I left?"

"and__?" prompted Sid.

"Err, I don't remember," replied Bert, looking a bit sheepish

"Make sure that the lodge were clean and tidy because we were going to lie low here after the job, until the heat died down and finally__ to stock the fridge and freezer with provisions. AND DON'T LEAVE ANYTHING PERISHABLE IN THE KITCHEN CUPBOARDS!!" he screamed, his little brown starry eyes nearly popping out of their sockets and a purple vein on the side of his temple swelling and pulsing.

Bert's face looked as red as a beetroot as he nervously turned and made a quick exit back into the lodge to wait until Sid had cooled down.

CHAPTER 10:
THE ESCAPE?

Macky forced himself up into a sitting position next to Tom, supported by the sacks of money. "The ropes around my wrists and ankles cut into my skin every time I move," he muttered.

"Yes, I'm the same," replied Tom. "I wish we could find a way of loosening them."

"What time is it Tom?"

"I wish I knew. Maybe if I turn sideways you could see the time on my wristwatch."

The watch had been given to him by his mother as a present for coming top of the class in the exams and now it was his pride and joy. The large circular white face with black roman numerals and the words Timex printed on the dial, could be seen clearly.

Macky twisted his head and leaned over Tom until he could see the watch face. "Blimey Tom, it's nearly 7 o'clock," he whispered, "we'll be losing the daylight before long."

"I wonder where the men are then. It's been ages since they left the van. Maybe they will never return and we will die in this rotten van," replied Tom.

He was becoming really agitated now. His mum, Uncle Billy and Aunty Nellie would be getting in a right state and they may never see him again.

They fell silent for a moment, each considering the options.

"I know what to do Tom," said Macky with urgency in his voice.

Macky quickly explained his plan, "You lie face down on the floor of the van and I will bite through the ropes on your wrists."

Tom hesitated. "Ok, then, but try to make it quick. The pain is unbearable."

Tom slid down onto the floor and rolled onto his stomach with his face pressed against the cold metal.

Macky lurched over on top of Tom and wriggled down until he could grip the rope in his teeth. Slowly he attempted to chew his way through the thick rope. "Ugh, this blinking rope tastes horrible," he gasped, spitting out bits of chewed twine.

"Keep going Macky," urged Tom, "the sooner you chew through the rope, the sooner I can release you!"

Macky returned to his task, with little enthusiasm. Tom was suffering now under the weight of Macky's body lying across him. Macky once again surfaced gasping for air. "I'm nearly through Tom. I'll have your hands free in a jiffy."

No sooner had he spoken the words when a sharp rattling noise came from the van door.

Tom looked up to see the weasel's face peering in through the open doors, "well, what have we here then, feeling a bit peckish are we?" he squealed, with a sickly grin on his face.

CHAPTER 11: THE FARMHOUSE

The fire had finally been extinguished. A few wisps of grey smoke rose from the burnt-out car. The car's doors and boot lid had been ripped off by the force of the explosion and now lay in the adjacent field. All that remained of the beautiful black limousine was a twisted metal skeleton, unrecognisable as a motor car and now ominously resembling an alien from deep space.

Police cars, ambulances and fire engines now filled the narrow lane. A police cordon had been placed across the lane where it joined the main road. A small crowd of locals stood behind the cordon whilst a police officer interviewed each person in the hope of finding out who owned the car.

Uncle Billy and Mary remained close to the scene of the burnt-out car. A senior police officer had informed them, much to their relief, that no bodies had been found in the wreckage. Uncle Billy's brain worked in overtime as unanswered questions raced through his mind.

Why did a fancy car come up a lane which only led to his farm?

What made the car crash and why did it catch fire so dramatically?

What happened to the occupant or occupants of the car?

The most worrying question was, WHERE ARE TOM AND MACKY?

His thoughts were interrupted by a shout from a rotund police officer strolling towards him. "Farmer Brown is it?" Billy nodded, "it appears sir that numerous bank notes have been found in the ditch and hedgerows a short distance from the wreckage," said the rotund officer. He continued after a short pause, "However, the most worrying aspect of the incident is that spent bullet cartridges have been found in and around the wreckage," he sighed.

Uncle Billy grabbed hold of Mary's arm to steady himself. "This cannot be happening," he murmured, "what if_ Oh my God no. What if Tom and Macky were walking up the lane, coming back home and say they came across something they were not supposed to see, and they were shot and killed!"

Mary's face was ashen as she began to weep.

"Calm down now sir," urged the police officer, "don't jump to conclusions at this stage of the investigation. Let's take this one step at a time."

Mary leaned against Uncle Billy, completely bewildered.

"We believe that the bank notes indicate the car could have been used in the bank robbery in town and that the robbers may have had a fallout over the money," said the officer. He continued, "Fortunately, the rear number plate of the car was found still attached to its boot lid. It appears from our records that the owner of the car had reported it stolen two days ago."

"But why was the car on fire and where are the robbers? More importantly, where are Tom and Macky?" Uncle Billy asked the officer, now completely exasperated.

"Well sir, we have officers searching all the surrounding countryside. A witness at the police cordon remembered seeing a small green van exiting the lane and speeding down the main road towards the village just after the explosion."

CHAPTER 12:
THE PRISON

The door required some tender loving care. It started its existence as a magnificent door, painted a subtle mint green colour with a superb gloss finish reflecting the face of anyone peering closely at it. Following many years of neglect and abuse, the mint green paint now discoloured by nicotine, had peeled off the door and hung down to form pale brown ribbons. Deep vertical scratch marks were etched into the lower surface of the door, made by the various pets that inhabited the home.

The old door stood at the bottom of a flight of rickety wooden stairs leading down from the ground floor of the lodge. A single light bulb swung from the ceiling on a flex, lighting up the small lobby area in front of the door.

Sid inserted a key into the large padlock chained to the door and unlocked it. With his left hand, he gripped the broken door handle, turned it and at the same time, gave the lower panel of the door a hefty kick with his right foot. The old door groaned on its hinges and slowly opened in submission.

Tom and Macky stood in silence, their hands tied behind them, looking into the inky darkness beyond the open door.

OK Bert, shove 'em in," snapped Sid. Bert pushed hard with the greatest enthusiasm, propelling Tom and Macky through the door opening, both staggering in the black void and finely collapsing on their knees onto a hard-concrete floor. The old mint green door slammed shut behind them, prisoners now in a tomb.

An eerie silence consumed the space. The darkness wrapped itself around them sucking away any hope they had of being found.

Macky fell onto his side uttering a low groan and then rolled over onto his back staring up into infinity. Tom edged along the concrete floor on his knees trying to figure out the size of the room. "Where are you Tom?" Macky muttered in despair, all his confidence now knocked out of him.

"I've reached a wall opposite the door. It feels like a brick wall and it must be about ten feet from the door." Tom pushed himself up against the wall until he stood on his feet. He inched his way along the wall until he reached the adjoining wall. He then turned and counted his steps until he came up to the facing wall.

"I reckon the room is about ten feet square."

"I don't know how that is going to help us, Tom. We are doomed," he gasped.

Tom didn't answer Macky, because his attention had been drawn to a pinpoint of light emitting from a position high up on the wall opposite him. "Macky, Macky, there's a tiny beam of light coming from the wall facing me," he whispered excitedly.

"I can't see any light," Macky retorted gruffly. "I'm lying on my back and it's all pitch black looking from my position."

Tom edged back across the space until he reached the wall facing him. He could now see a small crack in the wall at high level where the trickle of light came through. "Macky you've got to help me. I need to get higher up the wall to check this out." Macky groaned and shuffled back onto his knees.

"The only way this is going to work is for you to finish the job you started, Macky. So, bite through the rope on my wrists, then I can climb on your shoulders to see where the light's coming from."

"Tom, you need to keep talking or else I'll never be able to find you in the dark. My eyesight is terrible. I can't see a damn thing."

"Ok Macky, I am over here. Follow the sound of my voice." Macky began to shuffle on his knees across the hard floor towards the sound of Tom's voice.

Ouch! Crickey what the heck was that?" exclaimed Macky.

"What is it Macky, are you OK?"

"No, I'm not. I just knelt on something very hard and it sent a shooting pain up my leg," he shouted back, "oh, my goodness Tom, can you believe it. I just knelt on a blinking bone." Tom stood in silence now, trying to judge where Macky could be kneeling.

Blimey, this bone is really big. Feels like part of a human leg," he whispered to himself.

Tom moved cautiously towards Macky. He slowly swept his hand across the floor feeling for the bone.

Although they were both now within touching distance, they could not see each other in the inky black darkness. "Got it Macky," he whispered. "Gosh, you were right, it is a large bone." He could here Macky breathing heavily in the darkness, then he let out a gasp.

"Hang on Tom, I don't understand. I still have my bone in my hand," he exclaimed.

"Crickey Macky, what is this place?"

CHAPTER 13: BACK AT THE FARMHOUSE

Uncle Billy sat at the kitchen table, tapping his fingers repeatedly on its stained, wooden surface. "It's no good Nellie, the police haven't got a clue as to the whereabouts of Tom and Macky."

"Don't say that Billy, I'm sure somebody must have seen the green van on the road," replied Aunt Nellie.

"Well, the only good thing to come out of this terrible mess is that Tom and Macky must still be alive if they didn't find any bodies in the burnt- out car," said Mary, "they're probably travelling in the green van with the robbers," she concluded, with little optimism in her voice.

"Yes, perhaps we'll receive a ransom note from the robbers asking for money to release them," said Aunt Nellie.

Uncle Billy did not reply. Worrying thoughts were flying through his head. If the robbers have them it's not likely they will be released, even for a ransom, because they'll have probably seen their faces. Trying to find them now, would be like looking for a needle in a haystack. He kept his thoughts to himself.

"You will have to move from the table Billy, I'm going to bake some nice cakes ready for when they return," Mary stated.

Uncle Billy looked at her in bewilderment. "I don't think that is ___." The telephone rang, interrupting Uncle Billy. He raced into the hall and snatched up the receiver. "Any news?" he shouted down the receiver. Holding the phone tightly to his ear, he nodded his head frequently, while he listened intently to the voice on the other end of the line.

"Thank you, goodbye," he murmured, placing the receiver back on its rest. He strolled back into the kitchen deep in thought.

"Well, what was all that about then?" Aunt Nellie asked with excitement in her voice, "have the police found them?"

"Err, no not yet," replied Uncle Billy, "but the police say that they have received a call from a farmer who lives ten miles from our village. He reckons that he saw a small green van heading in the direction of the Wye Valley."

"Well, that's just great," said Mary sarcastically, "the Wye Valley covers an area of fifty miles and it's full of deep forests. How are the police going to find them there?"

"Listen Mary, they're going to have to start somewhere and this is as good as it gets at this moment in time," Uncle Billy replied in frustration, "the officer said that they will use helicopters and sniffer dogs, together with as many police officer as they can muster."

"Hey, that's right Billy, I've seen it on the tele, on those police crime serials," Aunt Nellie said, "If that fails, they bring in the army to search for the missing people."

"Thank you Nellie for your optimism, but I'm sure they won't go to those lengths just to find a missing schoolboy and tramp," Mary interposed. "I don't know that Mary, but I'm sure that if there's money involved then the bank will be giving a big reward to anyone who finds the robbers and the stolen money," replied Uncle Billy, "and if they find the money then they will find Tom and Macky." He hesitated and then sighed, "Hopefully."

CHAPTER 14:
THE MEETING
OF VILLAINS

A heavy fog had settled across the countryside in the evening dusk.

The car swung gracefully into the glade, the shafts of yellow tinted light from its headlamps slicing through the thick fog and lighting up the surrounding tree trunks standing like silent sentinels in the evening gloom.

The deep throbbing sound from the 4.5 litres supercharged engine of the magnificent 1930's Bentley Sports car suddenly ceased, the light beams slowly fading away, leaving the glade in an eerie silence.

The Bentley, its coachwork painted in a vibrant British Racing Green with its chromium spoked racing wheels, crouched perfectly still, shrouded by the thick hanging fog, like a Praying Mantis patiently waiting for its meal to pass by.

After a few minutes the driver's door of the Bentley gently opened, triggering the internal courtesy light to bathe its occupant in a soft white glow. Wearing a black trilby hat and a smart pinstripe double-breasted black suit, a stocky man with a large fat cigar clenched between his teeth, stepped out of the Bentley, his shiny black patent leather shoes squelching in the soft mud.

"S…t," he murmured, as the car door quietly swung closed behind him with a soft click.

Hunching over, he walked quickly towards the fuzzy red glow coming from the windows of the lodge. Stepping into the puddle, he uttered a veiled curse, whilst throwing his cigar away in disgust and climbed the steps to the lodge's veranda.

He removed his trilby hat to reveal a shiny bald head as he pushed the knackered door open with his shoulder and stood in the doorway surveying the scene in the cabin.

Sid and Bert sat facing each other at an old kitchen table. A red chequered, plastic tablecloth covered the tabletop on which bundles of bank notes were neatly stacked. A half empty mug of cold tea sat close to Sid's left hand. His right hand gripped the small shiny black revolver with the index finger curled around its trigger.

Bright red cotton curtains were drawn across the kitchen windows and a lamp with a battered red shade hung from the ceiling above the table. Cobwebs adorned the lamp shade.

The walls in the kitchen were covered in a grimy brown wallpaper. Fat droppings splattered the wall behind the cooker, adjacent to which stood a pale blue timber storage cupboard, its open door supported from one hinge, permanently exposing rows of baked bean tins. Numerous dirty pots and pans stacked in the sink's large basin climbed upwards towards the kitchen ceiling and standing in the corner of the kitchen, a small log burner spluttered and showered red hot sparks onto the timber floor through its open door. Opposite sat two well-worn dark brown armchairs, their stuffing bursting out.

"Funny smell in here," remarked the man, "it reminds me of kippers."

"Yer right Jack," replied Sid, "I thought that as well."

Bert sat in silence.

"OK lads, how much have we made today?" he asked, pulling up a chair and sitting at the table.

"Pretty good haul Jack for a few hours work," replied Sid, "we've counted £900,000 in nice crisp notes."

Jack nodded his head in agreement, "Well that's very good lads. We split one third each and then lie low for a while." Jack rubbed his chin with his right hand, deep in thought. Bert and Sid looked at Jack, patiently waiting for him to continue.

"The only problem could be," he said slowly to himself," is that the bank will have the serial numbers of the notes if they are all new. So, when we spend them, the police will find out where they came from."

Sid and Bert looked a little disappointed.

"Cor blimey, I never thought of that. What are we going to do then Jack?" asked Bert.

"Don't worry lads," reassured Jack, "we can launder the money, just like you do when you wash your dirty clothes and end up with clean clothes."

Sid and Bert remained silent, considering the proposal.

"But we can't go to the launderette with all this dirty money and clean it. It'll go soggy and anyway, someone will be bound to see us!" exclaimed Bert.

Jack and Sid stared at Bert, as if they were looking at a small child who was oblivious to what was going on around him.

"Bert," said Jack softly, "we are definitely not going to wash the money, I assure you. It is only a figure of speech. OK?"

Bert nodded slowly.

"So, what we do lads," stated Jack with confidence, "is this. I take the money to a bloke I know, who will move it abroad and give us clean money in its place, which won't be traceable," he added, "of course he will charge a small percentage for doing the work."

Sid and Bert both nodded as if in total agreement, not really understanding what Jack was talking about. They had worked with Cousin Jack on previous small jobs and had always trusted him with the money side, because of course, he was a bit brainier than them.

"Right lads, that's agreed then. I will contact the money launderer and make the necessary arrangements."

"How much will this bloke take for doing the job?" asked Sid.

"Probably about ten percent," replied Jack.

He carefully watched Sid and Bert trying to calculate how much they would finally get of the money on the table, "Which means you guys will take away a fantastic £270,000 each to spend on exotic holidays, luxury cars or even a grand house!" he exclaimed, throwing his arms into the air in a gesture of triumph.

Blimey!" screamed Bert, jumping up from his chair and doing a little jig round the table, "this can be our last job. I can live like a king for the rest of my life."

"Ok lads," continued Jack, "you must stay here for a bit longer, until the heat dies down. I will take the dirty money to my contact because nobody can associate me with the bank robbery. It is going to take a couple of days before I return with the clean notes."

"That's great Jack," Bert agreed, "we can wait a couple of days can't we Sid?"

Sid sat with a frown across his forehead and his eyelids narrowed to slits, "How do we know that yer going to return with the money, Jack?" he drawled, with a touch of suspicion in his voice.

The heavy silence could be cut with a knife. The crackling of the log burner penetrated the silence whilst Jack considered all his options.

He glared at Sid and realised from the look on his face that he would not back down. There was only one thing to do. "Ok, this is what we do then, "he continued, "I'll leave my share of the money with you and take your £600,000 with me to the money launderer."

Jack paused for a moment to see if they had taken the bait. Not a murmur from Bert and Sid. He pushed on, "I'll bring the clean money back to you and collect my £300,000 that I've left with you for safe keeping, just to show that I trust you both."

"That seems fair Sid," said Bert.

Sid slowly nodded his head," Alright then Jack, I agree.

"Jack counted £600,000 of bank notes and placed the bundles into the sacks.

Sid watched carefully to make sure that he took the agreed amount.

"What do we do with the two cretins in the cellar, Jack?" Bert asked.

Jack slowly turned to face Bert, "What two cretins?" he hissed between clenched teeth.

"The old geezer and the kid, Jack," Bert stuttered, "they were in the Merc when I wer waiting for Sid to arrive in the van."

"So, we had no alternative but to set fire to the Merc, tie 'em and bring 'em with us, cos they saw our faces," Sid spluttered out.

Jack stared at the brothers as if they were just dirt on his shoes, "I do not believe it. First you set fire to the Merc to draw attention to everyone in tarnation, then you miserable little creeps bring a couple of nincompoops back with you!" his face turning purple with rage.

"Hang on a minute, Jack," replied Sid, "don't forget that yer couldn't have pulled this job off without us."

"Yes, well without my brains and charisma you guys would still be washing pots in that grotty hotel," Jack said with a sneer, "who found the young lass that worked in the bank and persuaded her to show me around the bank out of hours, telling her that I was writing a book on a bank robbery," he laughed, "even managed to get the combination to the safe after a few gin and tonics at the local pub."

"Yes Jack, but__," Jack held his hand up. "No buts Sid. I spent a lot of my money setting this job up and I want payback now. I definitely don't want those two cretins hanging around when we abandon this shack."

"Ok Jack, we'll sort it out," replied Bert.

"That's right Bert, I'm sure you will. Take the gun and finish them off. Then bury them deep in the woods." Bert launched himself out of his chair, tipping it over in the process. "What me!" he exclaimed, "I've never killed anyone in me life."

"Well now's your chance Bert. Make sure the gun's loaded in case you miss them first time," he remarked, laughing out loud as he turned to leave, "give us a lift with these sacks, Sid." Sid picked up the gun from the table and placed it gently into Bert's hand, "Right then, off yer go Bert. I'll go and get a couple of spades from the garage."

With that, Sid picked up a torch hanging from a hook on the door frame and followed Jack out of the lodge with the sacks of money.

Bert stood dead still in the silence, completely paralysed with fear. The old cuckoo clock on the kitchen wall suddenly chirped the hour of midnight. Bert nearly had a fit and quickly responded by throwing Sid's mug of tea at it, scoring a direct hit.

The old cuckoo clock crashed to the floor uttering one last bleep, all its life having been beaten out of it. Slowly, breathing heavily, he walked to the kitchen sink unit, pulled open the drawer and took out the key to the cellar door. Turning, he advanced reluctantly towards the door leading down to the cellar, gun in his right hand, key in the other.

JACK MEETS SID AND BERT

CHAPTER 15: THE CELLAR

Kneeling in silence on the hard-concrete floor, they could both hear footsteps coming from the room above them.

"I reckon that this cellar has been used by the owner of the cabin as a kennel for his dogs," whispered Macky, "when we first stood in the lobby outside the cellar did you notice all the scratch marks on the paintwork at the bottom of the door?"

Tom quickly responded, "Yes, of course, I remember seeing them, but I didn't think much about it. But now you mention it, can you smell that horrible stench?"

Macky stared into the darkness, "You're right Tom. It smells like urine."

"We need to get out of here Macky, before we both suffocate."

"I reckon that crack high up on the wall's the frame of a window," replied Macky, "they would need to provide ventilation for the dogs."

"Ok then Macky, start chewing your way through the rope on my wrists."

"I can do better than that, Tom. This bone has a razor- sharp edge to it. I can have your wrists free in a jiffy."

Tom lay down on the floor, his face pressed against the cold concrete, with his arms behind his back. Tom kept talking so Macky could locate him in the darkness, "Don't take long, this is really uncomfortable."

Within minutes the rope snapped, enabling Tom to jump up and quickly remove the rope from Macky's wrists.

They both shuffled over to the wall where Tom had seen the chink of daylight, "I've lost it now," exclaimed Tom, "the light has disappeared."

"Don't worry Tom. The light has gone because it is night-time now."

"Oh no! How can we find the window now?" he uttered despondently.

"The window must be covered with some form of timber boarding. You must move along the wall until you can feel the timber. Now hop onto my back Tom, let's get going."

Macky leaned with arms outstretched, hands flat against the wall whilst Tom clambered up onto his shoulders.

Slowly they moved along the wall until Tom shouted to stop.

Tom's fingers made contact with the edge of a timber plank. He gripped the plank and tried to prise it off the window frame. The rotting timber crumbled away in his hands, "It's no good Macky. I've found the plank, but I can't move it."

"Come on Tom my boy, you can do it."

The timber plank broke into small pieces in his hands, the rotten timber showering down onto Mackys head, "I can't get a firm grip on the plank, bits keep breaking off when I try to pull it away."

"You must keep trying Tom, it's our only chance," he whispered in encouragement.

Just as Macky finished the sentence, a loud cracking sound resonated around the cellar as the timber plank finally submitted and fell from the window frame exposing a dirty pane of glass covered in cobwebs, "Well done Tom. Can you see anything?"

Tom swept the cobwebs away and rubbed the dirt off the glass with his jacket sleeve, "Below the window I can see grass and above it is the underside of the veranda," he gasped.

"The window must be at the front of the log cabin Tom. Can you see beyond the veranda?"

Tom pressed his face against the glass pane and squinted into the darkness beyond, "It's dark and a fog has come down. It's impossible to see anything." Pause. "Hang on. A light has been switched on and I can just make out a large green car parked near the cabin."

Macky's legs were starting to tremble now from bearing the weight of Tom on his shoulders. Oblivious to Macky's predicament Tom continued his running commentary, "The cabin door must have opened because I can see a big bloke walking towards the car. He's stopped at the car now and another thin man has joined him. It looks like Sid."

Macky remained silent whilst he listened to Tom. Holding his breath and trying with all his might not to let Tom fall.

"They are loading sacks into the boot of the car and now the big blokes got in the car. He's switched the headlights on and started the engine. I can see wisps of smoke coming from the exhaust."

Tom was so intent that he had forgotten all about Macky.

"Can you see the registration number of the car," Macky uttered quietly with his last gasp.

"Too far away in the fog. The car's moving and starting to turn around in the glade. Well, now it's reversing and coming towards the cabin. I can see the registration plate now it's lit up. Remember this Macky when I say it__. Here it comes, U P, U 2."

Macky nodded his head, forgetting that Tom could not see him in the dark, "great, the car is moving forward across the glade towards the woods. Lost the red taillights now in this rotten fog."

Macky shook Tom's legs, "You'll have to come down Tom, my legs are killing me."

Tom slid down his back and Macky slumped down to the floor, "What do we do now Macky?"

"Do you think that you could open the window and squeeze out?"

"Not likely. I'm not leaving you here and there's no way that you can reach the window."

They stood in silence, both alone in their thoughts.

CHAPTER 16:
UNCLE BILLY TO
THE RESCUE

The telephone only rang once as Uncle Billy instantly lifted the receiver, "What's the news constable? Please tell me that you've found them."

Uncle Billy listened carefully with his ear pressed firmly against the receiver, "ok, thank you officer for keeping us informed." He placed the receiver on the rest and returned to Aunt Nellie and Mary with a glum face.

"Seems that they have been searching near Dead Man's Wood. There are dirt tracks in the area which go deep into the woods and a vehicle can easily access them," he paused for a moment to get his breath and then decided to sit down, "the bad news is that they have called off the search because of the fog and are going to wait till morning. Better chance of finding them in daylight. If they are there," he added.

"That means they are going to spend a night in the cold with no food or shelter. In the depth of the woods where animals might be prowling," shouted Mary. She placed her hand to her forehead, "oh, my lord, this is terrible."

"Don't get hysterical Mary," Aunty Nellie spoke soothingly, "they could have found shelter in the woods. Macky is very practical and will make sure Tom is safe if they are there."

Uncle Billy suddenly stood up and strode with purpose into the hall.

"What on earth are you doing Billy!" Aunty Nellie exclaimed.

"If the police have given up searching for them, I haven't," he shouted dramatically as he pulled on his wellington boots and threw his Macintosh across his shoulders.

"Please be careful Billy, the fog is getting really bad," Mary cautioned as Uncle Billy lifted the telephone receiver and dialled a number.

After a short conversation, he turned to Mary, "I can't sit here anymore waiting for news, good or bad. I need to go to Dead Man's Wood and search for them. So, I'm rounding up the troops," He grabbed a double barrel shotgun from a cabinet, paused to check it was loaded and marched out of the farmhouse to the Land Rover.

Farmer Brown to the rescue!

CHAPTER 17:
THE ESCAPE

A chink of light penetrated the fog and shone through the window casting shadows on the cellar walls. Tom could just make out Macky's silhouette in the murky background.

Together in the silence, they heard heavy footsteps coming from the steps leading down to the cellar.

Macky gripped Tom's arm, "Someone's coming Tom," he whispered, "this could be our chance to escape. They think we are still tied up and can't see in the dark."

Tom's mind was in a whirl, "What can we do, we need a plan?"

Macky paused for a moment, considering the options, "Ok Tom. You stand facing the door and I'll be standing against the wall behind the door ready for when it opens."

Tom nodded and placed his finger to his lips.

Macky picked up a large bone and stood against the wall. They heard the key rattle in the lock.

Tom stood facing the door, his heart pounding in his chest, breathing heavily as the cellar door slowly opened, creaking and groaning on its rusty hinges. The light from the lobby spilled into the cellar bathing Tom in a soft glow.

Bert stood stock still, mouth open wide with the gun in his hand pointing directly at Tom. Recovering from the shock, he exclaimed, "What the hell's going on here then!"

Stepping into the cellar, Bert quickly swung the gun from side to side searching for Macky. Macky sprang out from behind the open door, arm raised holding the large bone, which he swung down swiftly onto poor Bert's head.

Bert didn't know what had hit him. In slow motion, he staggered forward, fell onto his knees and then finally collapsed face down, hitting the cellar floor with a satisfying thud.

The gun slipped from his grasp and slid across the floor.

Tom let out a gasp as Bert's face smashed against the concrete floor, "Crickey Macky, I think you've killed him."

Macky kneeling down, lifted Bert's hand to feel his pulse, "No Tom, he's still ticking along, must be made of tough stuff. He'll probably have a large lump on his head when he comes around. Serves him right, pointing that gun at you Tom," he concluded.

Macky retrieved the gun, popped it in his trench coat pocket and strode purposely towards the open door. They both ran up the stairs and across the lounge to the veranda door. Stepping out onto the veranda, Macky nervously looked around for Sid. He was nowhere to be seen.

The fog still hung heavy over the glade, making it impossible to find the entrance to the track, "Can you remember which way the car went Tom?"

Tom pointed straight across the glade, "I think it's over there." Tom walked slowly down the steps, avoiding the puddle and set off following the direction that the car had taken.

Macky followed close behind, his legs now aching from holding Tom on his shoulders.

CHAPTER 18: JACK TAKES A HOLIDAY

Emitting a deep throaty growl, the Bentley crept cautiously through the dense fog towards the woodland track. White, crystallised vapour plumes rose steadily from its three-inch diameter twin exhaust pipes.

Sid stood casually slouching, one hand deep in his pocket, the other holding the torch.

With a nasty smirk set across his face he watched the Bentley enter the woods, the fog swirling around it, leaving only the red rear lights and the illuminated registration plate visible.

As the car pulled away, Jack glanced through the rear- view mirror, slightly perturbed to see the smirk on Sid's face, "Ah well, I suppose that's a natural feature frozen to Sid's face," he muttered, dismissing the thought, "It's been a great experience working with you boys," he said, chuckling to himself as he thought of the £600,000 of crisp banknotes sitting in his car boot, "now then my little beauty," he said softly to the Bentley, "where shall we go? I fancy the South of France. Buy a nice little villa on the Med. Warm summers and mild winters.

That's the life for me!!"

He threw his head back and laughed so much that tears trickled down his cheeks as he weaved the Bentley along the tree lined dirt track.

Sid turned on his heels and strolled towards the garage to

collect the spades. Once inside, he switched on the garage light and opened the van's back door. Crouching down, he carefully dragged two large sacks towards him. With great effort, he slowly manoeuvred the sacks so that he was able to open each one.

Now breathing heavily, he muttered to himself, "What a brilliant idea of mine to skim £200,000 from the stack of notes on the kitchen table before Jack arrived."

So, it came to pass, that really there is no honour among thieves. The double, double cross had now been accomplished.

Gently sniggering, Sid tied the bags closed and pushed them back into the van. Slamming the van door closed, he picked his way through the debris strewn across the garage floor to a rack of garden tools fixed to the rear wall. He snatched the only spade from the rack and retraced his steps to the garage door. Switching off the light he stepped out into the fog. As he fumbled for the torch in his trouser pocket, he heard the lodge door creaking open. He was about to shout out Bert's name when he suddenly recognised two familiar figures walking across the glade away from the lodge.

CHAPTER 19: TO DEAD MAN'S WOOD

The battered old Land Rover rattled and lurched slowly down the country lane, leaving a trail of blue exhaust fumes. Behind it followed One Eyed Sid's father driving a small van with young Sid, Jack and Harry sitting in the back.

Uncle Billy coaxed the Land Rover along and quietly muttered, "Come on old girl, don't let me down now. We have to find Tom and Macky."

As the fog slowly began to disperse, he crossed his fingers and pressed the accelerator pedal down to the floor. In protest, two loud explosions came from the Land Rover's exhaust pipe, as it leapt forward and sped down the lane.

Uncle Billy stared intently as the Land Rover hurtled into the dark, unlit lane. The reflected light of the glass cat's eyes in the centre of the road, caught in the headlamp beams and flew towards him. He gripped the steering wheel so tightly that his knuckles turned white from the lack of circulation.

Through the fog he glimpsed the sign on the side of the lane indicating that he was approaching the Wye Valley. Touching the brake pedal of the land rover, he slowed to a walking pace, peering to the side of the lane in search of a turning into the woods.

Suddenly, in front of him, a large green car emerged from the woods and drove away at a fast pace down the country lane.

Uncle Billy braked abruptly, causing Sid's father to slam his foot down hard on the van's brake pedal. Hidden indiscreetly between the looming trees, Uncle Billy could see the entrance to a dirt track. He swung the Land Rover onto the track and drove cautiously into Dead Man's Wood, the van following closely behind him.

Finding it impossible to see only a few yards along the track, he stretched up and flicked a switch above his head. Immediately four large fog lamps fitted to the roof of the cab burst into life, flooding the track ahead in a crescendo of light.

CHAPTER 20: THE FINAL ACT

Although the fog had virtually cleared now, Macky and Tom found it difficult to find their way across the glade. The small amount of light coming from the cabin windows was soon swallowed up in the pitch blackness ahead of them.

The sound of a branch snapping stopped them both in their tracks, "Was that you Tom. Did you just step on a branch?" Before Tom could reply, they heard a swishing sound and the cold flat steel blade of a spade smashed across the back of Macky's head, felling him like a tree.

Sid stood over Macky with the spade in his hands, leering at Tom, "Now it's your turn laddie," he whispered. Tom looked down at Macky's inert body lying on the cold damp earth.

In panic he turned and ran for his life. Running blindly along the track in the ruts formed by the car wheels in the soft earth, his legs felt as if they were made of lead.

From behind, he could sense Sid gaining on him as the swishing sound from the spade grew closer, "Help me please lord!" he screamed, "someone please, please, HELP ME!"

"Yer will need more than the lord, yer little cretin. There ain't no way yer goin to get away from me now," laughed Sid.

Suddenly a brilliant bright white light pierced the fog in front of Tom and shone down on him. "This is the end for me, I'm going to heaven," was the last thought that flashed through Tom's mind as he collapsed into unconsciousness, completely exhausted.

Blinded by the intense glare from the Land Rovers fog lamps Sid stopped, spade raised above his head, frozen to the spot, "What the hell's happening?" he gasped in a haunted voice.

A large black, distorted figure, silhouetted in the light from the Land Rover, advanced slowly towards Sid. By its side were three small, black figures.

Dropping the spade, Sid stood petrified, mouth wide open with a look of fear on his face as he remembered the story told to him by Bert about The Child Snatcher, "They're coming to get me. Risen from the dead!" he screamed, as he slumped to the ground.

When Uncle Billy came into view followed by the three chums Sid could not believe his eyes, "Thank the lord," he gasped as Uncle Billy approached waving the double-barrelled shotgun.

"Right then mate, lie face down," Uncle Billy instructed.

Unfortunately for Sid the only place available for him to lie face down appeared to be the muddy tracks left by the vehicles.

Holding the shotgun in one hand, Uncle Billy took out a length of rope from his jacket pocket and passed it to Harry, "Ok then Harry, you're in the boy scouts so tie his hands behind his back." He then took a drinking flask out of his other jacket pocket, turned Tom over and sprinkled water onto his face. Tom suddenly spluttered and opened his eyes wide, "Uncle Billy! How on earth did you get here?"

"Calm down Tom, everything is going to be fine."

A muffled sound came from Sid, "Can I ger up now? This rotten mud's gettin up me nose."

Uncle Billy helped Tom to his feet and signalled for the boys to get Sid up.

Sid staggered up, face covered in mud, only the whites of his eyes and his yellow teeth visible.

A loud crashing sound came from the undergrowth as Macky suddenly appeared. Standing motionless behind Sid, he surveyed the eerie scene being played out in front of him, "Captain David Mackenzie of the 9th Battalion Royal Tank Corps reporting for duty sir." With that, he snapped his heels together and saluted Uncle Billy.

They all stood and stared at Macky in disbelief.

CHAPTER 21:
THE MEETING

They gathered in the lodge. Seated around the old kitchen table, the lamp with the red shade swinging gracefully above them in the gentle breeze coming from the open door. The table was stacked with bundles of crisp banknotes.

The fog had disappeared now exposing the new moon, shining so brightly that it covered the glade in a shimmering silver glow.

Uncle Billy sat at the head of the table. The shotgun cradled in his arms.

Macky and Tom sat to the left of him facing Sid and Bert on the other side of the table, Macky holding the revolver in his hand. The two villains sat with their hands tied behind their backs and ankles fastened to the chair legs. Bert's head rested peacefully on the tabletop.

Uncle Billy and Macky had to carry poor Bert up the steps from the cellar and deposit him onto a chair at the table. Suffering from mild concussion he then slumped forward and banged his head on the tabletop.

A large lump protruded through the hair on top of his head. Likewise, Macky gently massaged a lump below his woolly cap.

One Eye's father and the three boys sat on the floor in front of the log burner, casually throwing logs on to the fire.

Uncle Billy stared at Macky with a quizzical look on his face,

"Ok then Macky, let me get this straight," pausing to adjust the shotgun so that it pointed in the direction of Sid and Bert, "you are a captain in the 9th Battalion Royal Tank Corps and you've just been fighting a ferocious battle in France to liberate a town called Caen?"

Macky nods his head and Sid and Bert looked baffled.

Uncle Billy continued, "As I understand it, you are the commander of a Cromwell Cruiser tank, when suddenly, out of the blue, a German Panther Division opened fire on you scoring a direct hit on your tank?"

"Yes, yes that's right," interrupted Macky in excitement, "the tank caught fire, so I had to get my men out," he paused to catch his breath, "there was an explosion. The inside of the tank became an inferno, smoke and flames everywhere. I opened the turret hatch and shouted to my men to get out, but there was no response. All were dead."

Macky stopped to wipe tears from his eyes, "the heat was so intense that the hot metal on the turret burnt my hands. I flung myself into the deep snow surrounding the tank. My uniform and hair were on fire and I began to run for my life."

Silence, broken only by the creak of the lamp swinging on its rusty pendant.

Uncle Billy sits with a deep furrow across his forehead, his little white moustache twitching.

"So, when did this happen, Macky?" he enquired.

Macky thought for a moment, "Not long ago. I think it would be about February, because we had just celebrated Christmas at the army base on the French coast."

Tom just started to speak, when Uncle Billy suddenly coughed loudly, "Sorry Tom, I was just going to ask Macky what the year is now."

Macky responded quickly, "Daft question. 1944 of course."

Tom gasped, "Oh, my Lord," he thought, "it's OCTOBER 1951!"

Sid muttered to Bert under his breath, "This bloke's bonkers."

Bert just uttered a long groan.

Uncle Billy took control of the situation, "Well Macky, I'm sorry to tell you that the year is now 1951."

Macky looked bewildered, "It can't be," he paused, "Can it?"

"I think when Sid hit you on the head with the spade it caused a memory loss," stated Tom, "do you remember when we sat in the café you were writing in a notebook all about your dreams."

Macky sat staring at Tom with a blank look.

Tom pushed on, "Where is your knapsack Macky? We could find the notebook and read it to you. See if it jogs your memory."

"I don't remember the notebook Tom. It could be anywhere."

"It could be in the back of the van Uncle Billy."

"Ok Tom, you come with me and we'll search the van. You stay here and guard these two, Macky," with that, he placed the shotgun next to Macky, picked up the torch and walked out of the lodge. Tom hurriedly followed.

CHAPTER 22: THE REVELATION

They found the knapsack in the back of the van and to their surprise they also found two sacks stuffed full of loose banknotes.

Returning to the lodge, Uncle Billy passed the notebook to Macky and placed the sacks on the table, "What's all this then," he shouted at Sid and Bert.

Sid explained their little scheme and how they did not trust Jack who was their partner in crime. He also placed all the blame for the robbery on Jack, saying that they had been forced into committing the robbery against their will.

"Tell it to the police when we take you both in," laughed Uncle Billy.

Macky suddenly jumped up, dropping the notebook onto the table. Holding his head in his hands he started to weep. "This is terrible. It's driving me mad. I remember everything I told Tom in the café, but I still can't remember the person I was before the war," he sobbed.

"Yes, Macky told me that he had been so badly injured he could not remember his name, but he kept mumbling Macky in his sleep," declared Tom, "you see, he lost all his identification papers."

It was as if a fork of lightning had struck Uncle Billy, "I've got it! By Jove. I've got it!" he exclaimed, jumping up from the table to join Macky, "I've been sitting here, my brain in a whirl since you said that your name was Captain David Mackenzie of the 9th Battalion Royal Tank Corps." He continued excitedly, "the dates match up. Macky says that he was in France in 1941 and that he was so badly injured nobody recognised him. You lost your memory and identification papers. Your army unit back in England would have posted you 'lost in action, declared dead' and they would have sent a telegram to your relatives informing them of your death. I couldn't figure it out. You're a tramp with a memory loss, a long beard, a badly scarred face and permanently wearing sunglasses."

Uncle Billy paused for breath, "it would be difficult for anybody near to you to recognise you from a past life. Then it came to me like a bolt from the blue."

They all stared at him in complete silence, (excepting Bert who was away with the fairies.) each hanging onto every word that Uncle Billy uttered.

"Well, you could blow me down with a feather," cried Uncle Billy putting his hand to his forehead, "the name MACKENZIE shortened to MACKY! "

"TOM, SAY HELLO TO YOUR LONG-LOST FATHER!"

CHAPTER 23:
THE FAMILY

The warmth from the late morning sun slowly evaporated the dew lying on the meadows surrounding the farmhouse. A trickle of pale grey smoke rose casually from the farmhouse chimney, undisturbed in the still air.

"Oh, what a beautiful morning.

Oh, what a beautiful day.

I've got a wonderful feeling,

Everything's going my way.

There's a bright golden haze on the meadow__."

"For goodness sake Billy, give it a rest. You've been singing that song since we had breakfast." There was a trace of frustration in Auntie Nellie's voice as she sat on the old rocking chair, head in hands

"Now then dear, I just can't get it out of my mind. It's time now for us all to be happy and put all our worries behind us. We've had so much bad luck in the last few months."

Here, here," piped up Mary, busily kneading the dough on the kitchen table, "Billy's right Nellie. Now we have our family back together we can get on with our life."

Uncle Billy did a little dance around the table, his slippers gently slapping the flag floor, "How wonderful to have David home from the war. It will be his first Christmas with Tom. We can all open our Christmas presents ___."

A sudden crashing sound coming from the hallway interrupted Uncle Billy's rambling.

Tom in his excitement pushed the farmhouse door open so violently that it rattled on its hinges as it slammed against the wall and shook all the framed pictures.

Tom propelled himself down the hallway and into the kitchen, bumping into Uncle Billy as he completed his second circuit around the kitchen table.

"Steady on lad!" he exclaimed, losing his balance and grabbing the table to steady himself, "Why the rush? What's going on?"

Tom waving his arms in the air spluttered, "So..sorry Uncle Billy, but dads just arrived driving a fantastic, shiny green tractor!" he paused for a moment and then as an afterthought he shouted, "with big red wheels!"

"Come on then, let's go and have a look Tom," said Uncle Billy, grabbing Tom's hand, running together down the hall.

The brand-new tractor raced around the farmyard scattering the hens in its path as Macky wrestled with the steering wheel.

The tractor finally screeched to a halt in front of Tom and Uncle Billy.

Macky leapt down from the cab laughing with joy. He cut a fine figure without the beard and his hair cut short. He was dressed in smart, brown corduroy trousers, pale blue denim shirt and a black leather jacket.

"Well, what do you think Billy?"

Uncle Billy stood with a bewildered look on his face, "Blimey David. When I said go and buy a new tractor, I didn't mean a Rolls Royce tractor!"

"Come on Billy, you can afford the best now. This beast is a real workhorse and it will last us forever," Macky continued, "the reward money you received for nabbing Sid and Bert will set you up now and make your life easier and enjoyable. Don't forget also, that Tom remembered the registration plate on Jack's Bentley, so that the police were able to intercept him driving onto the ferry bound for France."

Uncle Billy slowly nodded, "Ok then, but I'm going with you when you go to buy that combined harvester," he chuckled.

THE END

ABOUT THE AUTHOR

Rex Denney

Hello Readers!

I was born way back in 1944 in a place called Bolton in the North West of England.

After completing school I went on to study for a degree in Mechanical Engineering at Mancaster University. I then spent my working life as an architectural consultant overseeing designs and constructions of all sorts of buildings.

I worked all the way up to 2011, when I retired aged 65.

When I retired my wife Sandra and I spent many a long weekend at a caravan in the Lake District, together with our grandchildren - Ruby and Sonny.

On our walks I would tell the children short stories that I had made up. They loved them and encouraged me to start writing children's stories, and so I set about putting pen to paper and ended up writing four stories over a number of years.

I have read each story to children at our local junior schools. Overwhelmed by their enthusiasm, I decided to publish the first of these stories - Macky The Tramp.

I'm now in my 80th year and so this is quite a leap of faith for me so I do hope you enjoy reading the story and thank you for choosing this book.